HZ

Please return/renew this item by the last date shown on this label, or on your self-service receipt.

To renew this item, visit **www.librarieswest.org.uk** or contact your library

Your borrower number and PIN are required.

4 4 0080074 7

Robert Dawson

Tuesday, Wednesday Quake Day

AUSTIN MACAULEY
PUBLISHERS LTD.

A CIP catalogue record for this title is available from the British Library.

ISBN 9781786295279 (Paperback)
ISBN 9781786295286 (Hardback)
ISBN 9781786295293 (E-Book)

www.austinmacauley.com

First Published (2017)
Austin Macauley Publishers Ltd.
25 Canada Square
Canary Wharf
London
E14 5LQ

Foreword

Yes, it's a nice medal isn't it? My name, look there –
Thomas Morrison – and there, Royal Humane Society.
I'm dead proud of it. I think it's solid silver. You should
get a picture of Nat with hers, too, cos we did it together
and she's got an award as well. Are you going to write it
down? Do you do shorthand? Oh, you're recording it on
the laptop – no, I don't mind.

One

Big Gran Lucretia predicted the earthquake. Nobody else was worried or even suspected, but she was the one who said there'd be trouble.

She was a Romani, see, and Romanies can tell what's going to happen. That's what they say, but I don't really think that's true. All Romanies *say* they can because it makes us sound mysterious but Big Gran really could.

There's a story told about her. She announced one day that a horse called Shark was going to win the Grand National and she told everyone the jockey's colours, but there was no horse called Shark running that year. There was one called Dolphin, though, with the right jockey strip, so everyone from our Traveller site put money on it to win. It didn't even get round the course and everyone was furious with Big Gran.

Two years later she told no one, but put all her cash – £100 – on a horse and this time it won and made her £10,000 and she used that money to buy special gold coins for all her Great Grandchildren. It was called Sharky.

It was about then that she told me about the earthquake, but I thought it best not to tell anyone. Well, she didn't say earthquake or I might have. She had this funny way of speaking. She said:

"Now listen, you 'ere young Blotch Morrison, dere's goin' to be trouble. You listen to your ole Big Gran." And she went on to say that there were men going to inject the earth with big needles and the earth wouldn't like being injected and would be upset and get very sore and start to shiver and shake with fever and everything on top of Mother Earth would shake and fall down. But to be honest, Big Gran was always saying stuff like that. After all, what did 'injecting the earth with big needles' mean, as if it needed a 'flu jab? And how could the earth catch a fever? She'd say, "I sort of seed it in my mind," and people would groan. Truth is, Big Gran had never been to school in her life and she couldn't read or write so I thought she had to be good at other things just to get by. Three of the things she was good at were working out what people were like, what might go wrong around her and how to plant ideas in people's minds. That's what I thought.

Lots of stories are told about Big Gran and how she could predict things and how brilliant she was at telling fortunes. As I say, I didn't really believe them. She told me stuff about what I would do in my life, but I'm not saying – it's too early to tell.

Mind you, there was another odd incident. She was out hawking one day – hawking, that's what the Romani women used to do in the past, selling bits and pieces door

8

to door – and she turned a corner in a road and there was a horse lying dead on the road, and its rider, a young woman screaming and crying. She asked if she could help but the young woman was too distraught. So Big Gran – she was a horse whisperer you understand – went up to the animal and lay herself part over it and whispered in its ear, then she put her hand in its mouth right to the back and next thing the horse was snorting and struggling to its feet. It was very distressed but Big Gran calmed it down and advised the young woman to walk it home, not ride, and give it a few days' rest and plenty of warm water to drink. The woman couldn't thank Big Gran enough. That wasn't all.

Two

You'll have realised we're Gypsy people, of course. We prefer to be called Romanies. Some people call us Travellers but that's not true because since we got this site to stay on, hardly any of the family have moved at all and certainly not Big Gran and the other Gran and old aunts. Big Gran's actually my mum's gran, and she's called Big Gran because Mum's mum is plain Gran, then we know which one we're talking about. It's not that she was physically big – well she was, but that's not why – but we sometimes say 'Big' as being more polite than 'Old'. She was big in our hearts and big in our lives.

So we're not Travellers. We're Romanies. Our families are important to us and we like to keep the old folk with us and not put them into homes, even when they go a bit divvy – I mean, senile.

Big Gran going on about injecting the earth didn't mean much at first, even though they were already pumping chemicals into it. I didn't think that it meant the same as 'big needles' and even when they started fracking over the far side of Beacon Ridge, the penny still didn't drop. Big Gran died a couple of years ago, so she never got to see what happened and I'm glad – though she obviously knew.

I'd better tell you a bit about this site where we live. There are sixteen pitches. That means there are 16 pieces of concrete where we can each park the trailer caravan we live in, and some people have a second smaller trailer which they use as a kitchen and sort of 'day room'. By each pitch there are three little brick sheds, one a bathroom, one a kitchen and one a storeroom. You want to try having a bath in the middle of winter – it's dead cold in there. But at least we've got somewhere safe. We have to pay the council every week just for parking on concrete and we also pay for electricity cards for the electric meters. It's my dad who collects the money to pass it on to the council cos he can read and write. There's no gas so we all use propane bottles.

Some sites are terrible and a few are run by gangs but we're lucky. If a gang takes over you have to pay much more and they put on their mates and criminals and you have to pay a sort of 'protection'. On our site, we're all related in some way, though sometimes it's very distantly which means we look after each other. The big snag is there's really nowhere for us to play on a site and vehicles are constantly coming on and off because with 16 pitches people are forever going shopping or doing work or coming back home so the road round the site is a danger to us all, especially to little ones who've nowhere else to ride their bikes or whatever.

It's true we did used to travel round, a long time ago. It was us Romanies did most of the fruit picking for farmers and collecting the vegetables or helping with harvests, but these days they've got machines or cheap foreign labour and, anyway, there's no place for us to stop any more.

Dad always wanted us to save enough money to have our own little site just for the family but the problem is you just can't get planning permission, even for four or five trailers. So that's why we're here on one that the council owns. The big worry is that the council might sell it to get rid of the responsibility and it could get bought by one of the gangs.

The illegal camping? Yes, I'll tell you. Mum says to answer any of your questions about Travellers 'cos we've nothing to hide. There are some Travellers who move about still and pull their trailers onto public parks and school playing fields and leave a terrible mess. Mum and Dad are dead against that. I know some haven't got much option, but it still shouldn't be places that cause problems for us all, as everyone thinks we're all alike then and we get the blame, too, but there are some who do it, Dad says, because they're up to no good and actually have a home somewhere, like some of those Travellers with big properties in Ireland and scattered round the mainland. I'm going to prove to you that we're good people.

Three

From our Traveller site, you get a good view of Marshall Meadows. If you stand on top of the earth banking which runs almost all round the site – which is to stop the house-dwellers having to look at the Gypsies – you get the best view. Huge tanker lorries and other lorries loaded with massive drums, which are then injected under pressure into the ground. It had to go very deep in case it affected the pure drinking water supply. Actually, mostly they drilled and sent it almost two kilometres under the earth and they said it would be safe there.

No one was quite sure what the chemicals were. I suppose the people who put it in there knew but they didn't announce it. All the sign said was, 'Danger, Keep Out'. There were pictures of skulls and crossbones everywhere.

There was also the dust. Clouds of it, which settled on every bit of the site, day and night. It didn't matter how much you hosed the trailer down, a couple of hours later it all looked sandy coloured, but as Mum said, it was somewhere legal to stop.

I found out the hard way what the drums contained. When I was little and new on the Traveller site, I went to investigate one evening. Dad was collecting scrap metal and selling it on then and I thought the empty steel drums might be stuff to recycle for a bit of money (actually, I now know they're rarely worth the bother even if they're clean ones). I suppose it was pinching really, but I didn't think of it like that. I should have realised that, if it had been safe, the men folk on the site would have had them long before.

So one day, I picked my way between two strands of the barbed wire fence and crossed a patch of grass to the cinder track which runs from the entrance gate of Marshall Meadows over to the huge drill things. Next to the track was a stack of empty drums waiting to be collected, some of the black stuff having spilled on the ground. I left the track and squelched into the black stuff to pick up one of the drums to take back to the site. The black ooze felt slimy and slippy and I had to waggle my toes in my boots to stop myself from slipping. Suddenly, I saw that my boots had begun to smoke and fizz, only a little at first, but then my feet started to feel hot. I staggered back to the cinder track and tried to yank the boots off. But that got the stuff on my hands and it started to burn straight away. I was screaming in agony and one of the workmen heard me and rushed up to me. Of course, he was in protective clothes.

They started washing me with cold water, which was scary in itself, and one went and ran for Mum. Using all that water might have saved my life and it stopped the burns being even worse, but bad enough to lose the skin from my feet and hands and a bit on my face where I'd touched myself with the burning hands.

They grafted skin onto me at the hospital and it was awfully painful. It took lots of weeks and I cried a lot. All the time Mum stayed with me. My hands and feet looked twisted and out of shape, though they got them straighter, but at least I was still alive. People could see the blotches on my hands and legs and my face, they just weren't as bad as they might have been.

That's how I got my nickname of Blotch.

That's also what made me realise how dangerous Marshall Meadows could be. One thing the company learned, they put up a much bigger and stronger barbed wire and netting fence all around the site so it's almost impossible now to get into there except through the official gate – not that I've ever wanted to try. Trouble was, as things turned out, we weren't sure if my little sister also knew the danger.

Four

The day it happened, I'd set off in a bad mood 'cos they'd made me take Luckry to school. She's my little sister – of course you know that – and she was dawdling like she always does. Yeh, I know it sounds a funny name but that's what we call her, a sort of nickname like I'm Tom instead of Thomas (my dad) and she's Luckry instead of Lucretia (my great gran). Travellers use a lot of nicknames or shortened names and there are even people about who have genuinely forgotten their real names.

For the third time, I asked her, "Try to walk faster than that," I sighed, and immediately regretted it. "We're late, see, sis, and there's still a long way to walk."

"OK, Blotch!" Luckry answered cheerily.

It wasn't true – yet – but I just felt that way. It really was too bad having to walk her to school in the first place, yeah and I admit I resented it. She and I are the only youngsters who go to school from our site and there are no school buses our way so when Mum can't take us, we have to walk.

We turned into the main road leading to town. "Hi, Blotch!"

I hadn't seen my classmate Nat Walker till she caught us up in the middle of one of the crossings.

"Hi, Luckry!"

"I like your hair," said Luckry, and I noticed that Nat's straw colour plaits were fastened against her head which is the way some Traveller girls have them, too. I hadn't noticed until then.

"Thank you ," she said.

Luckry gave a shy smile back. "Tom's grumpy," she whispered.

"I am not!" I protested, wishing I could make her disappear. "It's just ..." I began.

"Just what?" Nat slapped me on the arm. "Come on you old grump, just what?" I wouldn't have taken that from anyone else.

"It's been one of those days," I sighed.

"Been? It's hardly started. You're not even at school yet."

"It's her."

I glanced down at my sister's black plaited hair, shining in the sun. In her blue and white checked gingham dress she looked almost doll like. I remembered how helpless she really was and how we Romanies set such store on looking after young children. I decided to try to be much kinder for the rest of the journey to her school.

"I'm sorry. I'll tell you the truth. I didn't want to walk her to school, And yeah, she's right, I keep sounding grumpy."

"No mum or dad to run you in the tranny today? Poor you! I wondered what'd got your legs working," Nat chuckled.

I shook my head. "They're out for the day. Dad's gone to get spares for the motor and Mum went for the ride. I wanted to go, but they said I had to go to school. So I ..."

"I get the picture. And poor little Luckry gets the short straw and you're riding shotgun for her. And Henry Morgan Secondary only right next door to her primary school, too. Now that's what I call really tough."

"OK, OK, back off. I know, I'm out of order."

We walked along London Road in silence. Ahead, the stone and marble walls and pillars of Shawville's council offices shone in the morning sun. Traffic had already built up and the roads, smaller than those of a larger town or city, were crowded. Away from the residential areas, the streets of the town squeezed through 19th century stone buildings. Several main roads radiated from a huge traffic island at the edge of the town. Henry Morgan Secondary and Henry Morgan Primary Schools nestled on a site at the far side of the main island.

A large chemical lorry, presumably trying to avoid the jams on the bypass, crawled down the road on its way to dump on Marshall Meadows. It threw up a cloud of dust.

"Oi!" Nat roared back at it. "Dust all over." She stopped, knocking dust off the Morgan Secondary uniform of grey jumper and slacks.

"New on today," she complained. "I got stuff in my hair, too?"

I peered at the straw-coloured plaits tied to the sides of her head. "No, I don't think so."

Nat slapped at my similar uniform. "The muck mostly missed you," she said.

"Makes a change from the site," I said.

We walked on.

Five

"So why else is it a bad day?"

"What?"

"You said, 'it's been one of those days'. What else went wrong?"

"A dog kept him awake <u>all night</u>!" Luckry chipped in.

"What, <u>all</u> night?" Nat teased.

"It felt like that. Yap, yap, yap."

As if on cue, we turned the corner into the main road, and came across a persistently yapping dog.

"Shut up!" I snarled.

The dog stood there, insistent, nagging, wagging its scruffy tale ten to the dozen as if inviting us to have a game with it.

"Good doggie."

Before I could stop her, Luckry leaned forward and patted the dog on its head. I had visions of its fangs ripping at her hand and all the problems that would cause – Luckry screaming the place down and Mum's reaction back home. Mum's parting words as we set off: "Look after her, she's your responsibility."

"Poor doggie!" she said. "It's lost its mummy!"

"It'd lose its voice if I had my way," I muttered.

Another huge tanker lorry approached. We all leaped to one side away from the pavement edge and I couldn't hear Nat's response. I yanked Luckry back.

"Sorry," I said instinctively.

"We saw our hens running all over the place," Luckry told Nat excitedly, trotting to keep up. "They were playing chase and flapping their wings and clucking and going back and forth and round and round."

"They're thick," I countered. "Like that dog. Charging about in a pen like a fox'd got in amongst them. Stupid things."

"Yeah, you sure are grumpy!" Nat slapped my arm again. "Pull out of it. Is everything going to upset you today?" I like Nat a lot, though she's not a girlfriend. Really I think I'd like it if she was, but I've no chance with a non-Gypsy girl because everyone at school'd persecute us both to death. It would be just the sort of ammunition they need.

"Sorry," I said simply. I knew she was right, I bit my tongue and took to thinking about the morning. I was aware of Luckry telling Nat every last detail of the hens incident.

"Hens and dogs!" I said aloud. "What is it about them?"

"What?" Luckry asked.

"Oh nothing, I was just trying to remember something, that's all."

But remember what? Why was it that barking dogs and flapping hens rang alarm bells? Something silly, I was sure.

I pushed the unanswered question to the back of my mind. It was something to do with school, so it couldn't be anything important or I'd remember, I decided.

Traffic was building up far more now on the town's streets, crawling towards the snarl-up of the town edge island.

"Blotch?" Luckry's voice interrupted my thoughts.

"What?" I deliberately made my reply short and sharp, suspecting she was probably about to ask me something silly and hoping it'd stop her.

"You know my pumps?"

"Not personally."

I was aware of her face looking up at me, puzzling over my answer.

"You're at it again," Nat warned.

I nodded an apology.

"I can't fasten them."

I almost said 'Tough!' but stopped. "There's nothing I can do about it, sweetie," I said, trying to sound

22

reasonable. "I can't go in the lesson with you. You'll just have to learn and do your best and the teacher'll help you. That's why Mum bought you tie-ups so you'd learn how to do it."

Luckry's big eyes looked up at me. "You see, I always knot them when it's PE and I take them off. Then next time they're still in a knot and I can't do them."

"Just say to the teacher, 'I can't tie them, they're knotted, please will you help,'" Nat advised.

"I do, only they're <u>always</u> knotted, see and it makes her grumpy and she says she hasn't time. Will you show me again how to get knots out and tie them so they don't?"

"But your pumps are in school and we haven't time. Sorry."

I tried to ignore Nat's glare.

Six

At the large traffic island, which we had to cross, Luckry halted. A tug at her hand only made her stagger and pull harder against me.

"The well!" she said. Then I remembered. It was one of those silly rituals which the family had. Every time we walked anywhere near the well, even shopping in town, Luckry had to make a wish. It was a lucky well, as the sign said, 'Mother Maria's Magic Wishing Well.'

"I want to wish! I always wish!" she pleaded.

"No," I said. "There isn't time."

She began to cry. "But Big Gran says we MUST," she sobbed.

I glanced at Nat. She didn't seem to mind the sudden halt.

"You want to wish?" Nat asked Luckry.

"Yeah, I always used to. Wish for something good, though."

I searched my pockets and found a coin.

"I've got one from my money pig ," she said. "It's a big wish."

"Hurry up," I pleaded. I gave her hand a tug, but I must have tugged too hard as she overbalanced. I half caught her so she didn't actually go down but she twisted and knocked her knee on the side of the well wall.

"Ouch!" A little tear misted her eye. I bent and looked at the knee which had the tiniest of grazes. I gave it a healing kiss and in her mind it did the trick.

"Be gentle with her, grump. Wishing's special when you're only six and one day you might be sorry you were so bad tempered with her," Nat fired.

Luckry tossed the coin in and peered over the small wall and through the lattice grill to watch it hit the water. I heard it plop.

"Hey!" she said. "That's funny! Mother Maria's making a cup of coffee."

I ignored her, and turned my back to the well in contempt as she stood there, eyes closed, wishing, almost as if praying.

"You done all your homework?" I asked Nat.

"Yeah, for once," she answered simply, and turned to Luckry. "What you say, sweetie?"

Luckry pointed at the well and at the same moment, I heard the strange plopping sound again. I peered over as I grasped her hand. Now I saw what she meant. The water was bubbling, like an overfilled kettle. I thought I could see a pound coin and I guessed it was the one Luckry had just wasted.

"Hey!" I said. "That's odd!"

"Yeah!" Nat agreed. "Sure is! Must be something disturbing it somehow!"

"She's making a cup of coffee," Luckry repeated. "Shall we wait and watch?"

"No! And where did you get that coin from?"

"I told you. My money pig. Big Gran told me to."

I sighed, "Luckry, Big Gran died just after you were born, so she can't be telling you things. We've had this conversation lots of times before."

She turned her big brown eyes towards me. "She did, she talks to me quite often sometimes and she says when you say things like that to take no notice. She told me to get the big gold coin from my money pig and take it with me today and chuck it in the well. Then I had to wish for something very big to help me."

I hardly heard what she said. I was feeling very snappy not so much at Luckry but because I didn't understand these odd things yet I knew I should. Was the world going mad? Why was water bubbling? What with that and the dogs and the hens ... What was it?

A man carrying an old-fashioned billboard wandered past. I noticed the advert. 'The end of the world is nigh.' And on the back, 'So see it through with a cup of coffee at World's End Café.'

"Try Mother Maria's!" Nat called after him. He held up one finger to her and I saw a flash of anger cross her face. I realised that if we hadn't been on our way to school and hadn't had Luckry with us, that man would have felt her wrath. He shouted something back at us. I couldn't quite get what, but it was about taking better care for the little girl with us so he must have seen her stumble.

I smiled. "Come on!"

"Do you want to know what I wished?" Luckry asked as she scampered to keep up.

"You mustn't say," Nat intervened. "Otherwise it won't come true."

"Keep it secret!" I added. "All I want is to get you to school in one piece and to remember ..."

"What?"

"I dunno, oh nothing."

I stopped, thankfully, as we reached the gates of Luckry's school.

It was a single-storey building, first built in stone over a century ago, before the town grew. Later extensions were of cheaper bricks and concrete, when money was scarcer. Two steps led up to the entrance, with a disabled ramp alongside, and old-fashioned looking wooden entry doors.

"Now you go straight in," I ordered. I buzzed the security and drove her in. "The others are already inside."

She reached up on tiptoes and tried to kiss towards my face. My heart softened slightly and I let her brush-peck my cheek and gave her a good kiss back. "Good luck with the laces!" I smiled.

"What are you trying to remember, then? Always to be nice to your sister?" Nat asked as we watched Luckry run into her building. We turned towards our own school, a couple of hundred metres or so further along the road. We were already nearly late, but ours started fifteen minutes after Luckry's.

I shrugged, "I don't know. It just seemed odd. Damned dogs barking, hens going crazy, the water bubbling! It rings a bell somehow."

"My God!" Nat said. She stopped in her tracks and slumped against the wall. "My God!" she said more softly, as if the words were so shocking they were repeating themselves. "I hope you're wrong!"

"Why?" She'd alarmed me.

"Don't you know? It's a disaster waiting to happen. That's always the signs – oh my God! They're coming – it's the invasion of the green Martian slime balls!"

She slapped my arm again and laughed.

Seven

I glared at her. "I didn't mean it about the slime balls, you know," Nat sniggered.

"I know that, I'm not stupid."

"So why the long face? You've got shot of Luckry, poor little kid."

I gave a huge sigh. "I suppose I was a bit snappy with her. But you know I'd give my right arm for my kid sister. No, it wasn't that. There's something – something, sort of, nagging at me."

"It's your conscience – if you have one." Now Nat sighed. "Oh, sorry, that was mean cos I know you have really." She slapped me.

"I wish you'd stop doing that. I know it's only fun but your slaps'd knock out a professional boxer. If you were a boy I'd floor you ," but it was a silly thing to say as Nat's the sort of girl can look after herself. If I'd retaliated, I'd probably have come off worst but in any case I could have lost a good friend. "No, it's something to do with the dogs and the hens and the water bubbling. It's reminding me of something. If I could just remember what. Something worrying, something awful."

"Like missing the football match on TV, I suppose." Nat's voice became creepily soft. "Course, it could really be the slime balls, eh? Imagine them, touching your hands, slipping over your face to stop you breathing."

I glanced into her face. She was smiling, but it was a teasing smile.

I sighed. "Yeah, sure. Maybe you're right. Maybe it's just conscience about Luckry. But she can be such a pain."

"And I suppose you weren't at her age?"

She was right and it didn't seem worthy of an answer. We reached the steps to the main entrance to our school. The main building has three floors. On top of the roof stood a now ornamental bell tower. When the stone school was first erected, the bell rang to tell students it was time to come for their lessons. Now it acted as a landmark in the area.

My and Nat's classroom was in this main stone building, and on the ground floor. The upper floors were almost exclusively classrooms for those slightly older than us Year 10s.

I noticed a flock of pigeons wheel lazily in the sky, descending towards the now distant elementary school building, then at the last moment rising again, as if they'd just discovered the building wasn't there at all.

"And I expect you could fasten your own laces before you were even born," Nat sniped.

The buzzer went for the last warning for the start of school. "Come on," Nat urged. She tugged my arm to speed me and there wasn't time for me to fire back. We ran past the last two of the flowering cherries, which decorated the edge of the main school car park, and took the flight of steps at the main entrance, two at a time.

I was late in class, and Mrs. Anderson was already checking the registrations.

I mouthed an apology to her, and took my usual seat.

When she'd finished the register, I noticed that Ellie Connors had her arm up, to attract attention.

"What's the matter, Ellie?" Mrs. Anderson asked.

I hardly listened, until I heard her mention that all the goldfish lay dead in some garden pond. She was asking for the cause, and then she added, "And the water was, kind of, bubbling."

"Hey – I've seen that too! The wishing well in town," I blurted. "The water there, sort of plopping!"

And realised my mistake.

"Been wishing?" Mark Jacobs called. "Travellers can't look human."

I turned to snap, but Mrs. Anderson quietened the class before I could. Others of my classmates reported odd sightings.

"You should've seen the rats in town this morning," Charlene Hughes shouted enthusiastically. "Huge fat ones, running from building to building, like they were scared."

"They must've got a cat there," Kath Drew chipped in.

"Or they saw Gyppo blotchy boy!" sniggered Mark.

I didn't take the bait this time because something about the rats rang another bell in my head. Deserting a sinking ship, that was it. Like the birds which wouldn't land.

"Anyone see those pigeons?" I asked. "They were kind of odd, too."

"Yeah, and dogs going daft," Charlene added. "Ours howled all night."

"Ours did too," said Ellie.

"So would I if I lived with you," Martin shouted.

A new voice. "I know what it is." The voice was calm and full of authority.

Eight

But the whole class still moaned as one at Richard Shearer's voice. "It's obvious. Don't you remember, in Personal and Social Education class, the environmental damage?"

The moan increased. Richard knew everything, or thought he did.

"Let him speak!" Mrs. Anderson snapped.

"It's an earthquake."

The whole class subsided in laughter. Two show-offs collapsed on the floor for added effect.

At last Mrs. Anderson regained order.

"Be quiet! Listen to Richard."

I noticed a smile playing on her lips and guessed she expected something foolish.

"That's what happens just before an earthquake. It's well documented."

For a moment, the sheer shock took the wind out of my lungs. It hit me far harder than the heaviest of Nat's blows. Now I remembered where I'd heard it, too, and Richard was right. That was exactly what'd been said in PSE when they'd been discussing the ethics of Marshall Meadows and what I'd been trying to remember all morning.

"Nonsense. There's never ever been one here. Britain isn't the sort of place which has earthquakes and if there'd ever been one, history would tell us, so we'd know if there had been. There can't be," Mrs. Anderson said coldly. "We're not even on a fault line."

There was the typical class snigger. "But Mrs. Anderson," Richard continued, "don't you see? It's not normal fault lines. It's the chemicals they're injecting into Marshall Mountain which are causing it and who knows – maybe the fracking is a factor as well."

Someone else joined in. "Remember in Citizenship? Denver in the USA? They'd never had one there, either, till they pumped stuff into the ground. It caused a quake – pillars in a church cracked, so did floors, windows broke, furniture fell over and a chimney fell and smashed into a car – and that was only a little 'quake. Remember that?"

I half wanted to believe and half wanted for it to be proved nonsense. Someone said, "This isn't Denver and that was years ago. We've learned about things like that since. Looking after the environment and all that stuff."

Richard shook his head. "But we haven't learned. We're still doing it. Just look at Marshall Meadows. I can remember playing there when I was a kid, but look at it now, all fenced off with huge walls and razor wire."

I thought of my gnarled feet.

"Hang on!" Nat interrupted. "The Meadow's only a dump, that's all it is. Yeah, it's waste chemicals, but they're very careful. That's why they're putting them there, because it is environmentally safe. There's no streams underground, nothing to let the chemicals leak out. That's why they use it. And drilling down to inject the stuff in couldn't be safer. It just lies there in holes and harms no one."

Richard shook his head more violently. "You're wrong, it is a 'quake coming. That's all it can be. They don't just inject the chemicals in holes. It's like a dentist; they drill a hole, put in the filling and put a top on. But they don't just push the chemical in; they pump it in as liquids under huge pressure, then ram the plug back. It's like putting fizzy pop in a bottle. The top won't come off, only this bottle has a weak base! Don't you see? It's about to crack!"

Nine

Mrs. Anderson smiled. "Nice one, Richard. "You almost had me believing you. Right class, enough fizzy talk – if you've got everything, it's time you went for your first lesson.

I wanted to shout, "Don't you see? He's right! It is an earthquake coming. It's the chemicals they're injecting into the mountain causing it – the animals and everything else are the signs. Richard's right!" But I said nothing. Why not? Well, it's difficult being the only Traveller boy in that school. The other Traveller kids of secondary age just never went and I envied them but my parents made me because they said they wanted me to make something of my life. It'd been really rough at first as I had to take a lot of teasing, like 'The Black tinker will get you,' and pretending I had some awful disease, or calling me 'Gyppo the thief' or 'Pikey boy' or touching me and then wiping their hands because touching me supposedly made them dirty. That's why I valued Nat's friendship so much. She was the sort of girl who'd call a spade a mechanical digger.

There was another thing helped me. There was a kid there older than me used to be on our site – he's at uni now – and unlike some of the Romani kids, his parents made him go to school as he's nearly a genius. He ended up with fourteen O levels and four A star As and he's good at sport, so the other kids began to accept him, and I got the reflected glory and it made it better when I was the only Romani boy in school. I'll be gone before Luckry comes so I wouldn't be in her shoes.

Anyway, Mrs. Anderson gave Richard a smile of slight amusement and pity. "I don't think you need worry about earthquakes, class. As I say, we're nowhere near an earthquake area let alone a fault line. We're …"

But I couldn't contain myself any longer. "But don't you see Mrs. Anderson? It all adds up. The dogs and things. Shouldn't we evacuate the building now, and warn the primary school staff?" Lots of people sniggered and the show-offs did another collapse in a heap.

Richard nodded his head vigorously, trying to persuade her. I looked to Nat for an opinion, but she was studying something on the table in front of her, as if it was the most important object in the entire universe, and so deliberately avoiding my eye contact. Several kids moaned and I heard someone say something about Gyppos injecting themselves with the Marshall Meadows poison.

Mrs. Anderson smiled again. I recognized it as a pitying one. "Dogs you say? Acting oddly? Take a look."

She pointed vaguely out of the window. The whole class, as if on command, stood and turned to peer from the window.

I recognized the scruffy mongrel dog we'd met on the way. It ambled across the recreation area. It looked so at ease, you could almost imagine it humming to itself. It reached a flowering cherry tree, stopped, sniffed delicately, and cocked its leg.

"It doesn't look so worried to me," Mrs. Anderson said, with a type of smile which I recognized as meaning 'Don't be foolish any more.'

I sighed. I thought of Luckry in the neighbouring school. Was I being stupid and worrying about nothing? But what if Richard <u>was</u> right?

The class sat down again and began sorting things for the day's lessons round the building. Books and files moved in and out of bags, ready to do the tour. I could hear the gabble that Mrs. Anderson was right, and the whole idea was crazy.

I did try to convince myself I was wrong. It was true; there were no fault lines anywhere near so earthquakes weren't possible. And even the Denver one with the chemicals wasn't <u>that</u> bad.

But I just couldn't convince himself. Too many odd things had occurred. And there was Luckry, stuck in that primary school. *If something did happen* ... I couldn't hold the thought. It was too horrible.

Mrs. Anderson was making some sort of announcement about a trip and we hadn't to forget to sign our name on the list if our parents said we could go. It was to go to the fresh water reservoir, called Devil's Hole because it was said to be so deep it went right down to hell in the middle (as if), about two miles north of our site. It's a sort of medium sized reservoir but big enough for us to do yachting and canoeing. I wanted to go but I'd forgotten to ask Mum and Dad and it was a tenner to go, which is a lot to us.

My mind drifted to the dog which hadn't shown any sign of being bothered and dogs knew these things. Stupid, everyone knows you don't have earthquakes in England, do you?

I glanced through the window. I could see the dog still there, in the middle of the recreation area, only it wasn't walking any more, it was cantering, round and round in a big circle, like a runaway engine on some sort of track, round and round, as if it had gone mad.

Ten

Then I knew – or thought I did. I was as sure as the sun rises. There was a quake, it was on its way, and the dog *was* the final proof. I put up my hand to warn everyone. My eye caught something moving near the ceiling. It was the class globe because this was a geography room. It turned slowly, like the real earth spinning. Its very slight swing, from side to side, reminded me of a failing pendulum clock, one with the hands almost striking midnight.

The globe spun the opposite way to the earth. For no more than a dozen seconds, I wondered about the consequences in real life if the sun rose in the west, and set in the east.

But the wobble ...

"Mrs Anderson!" I put my hand up only to point at it.

She glanced where I pointed.

"I don't think that's very funny, Thomas. I saw you knock it," but I hadn't.

"It's a ghost!" Martin Jacobs joked, and several people sniggered. I felt like sloshing them. They were too stupid to realise what was happening.

Richard shouted, almost screamed, "A 'quake is coming – will you listen!"

"This 'quake gag's gone far enough. It's time you were moving to the first lesson, and I'll have no more time wasted by you, thank you."

"But Mrs. Anderson …!"

"Enough, Richard! Up to your first lesson."

All round him, people stood, pushing back chairs. I felt the vibration of them as they scraped across the floor.

Something metallic rattled a couple of metres behind me, like loose change in a tin. I didn't know what it was but Mrs. Anderson glared beyond me.

From the edge of the room, came a sound like a giant insect scrunching and a window rattled as if a big chemical lorry had just passed – except they didn't come this way – and the faint rumble of the chairs being pushed back hadn't stopped, but no chairs were moving!

"Mrs. Anderson!" Someone called uncertainly over to her.

"It's only the central heating," she said. "Nothing to worry about, only an airlock. Enough time wasting, hurry along to the first lesson, because you're already late."

Now strange things began. Charlene and several kids staggered over by the outside wall. It was such an odd sight, like they were on the deck of a ship.

Mrs. Anderson looked puzzled. "Perhaps, er, well maybe …"

She was stuck for words. Everyone could see.

"Mrs Anderson!" I shouted.

The people who'd almost fallen came back, looking confused, and sat silent at their tables as if they'd all been programmed as morons.

Martin said, "Shut up!" to me, but only to me.

Something – it came from near the doorframe – groaned, like a skeletal tree in a spooky film.

"Mrs. Anderson!"

My shout was far more forceful now, easily out-sounding the questioning mumbles of my classmates, but two or three others gave little screams of fear and doubt.

"Mrs. Anderson, we must do something!" This from Richard.

There was a sudden crack, like a gun, and one of the classroom windows cracked straight across.

Several kids screamed.

I looked beyond the crack and outside. The dog was still there, running in a smaller and faster circle now, as if chasing a very long tail and howling like a demented ghoul.

The tree against which it had relieved itself only minutes before shook as if trying to throw off the dog's urine.

"Mrs. Anderson, we must get out!"

She stood at the front of the class, bewildered, in a dream turning steadily into a nightmare.

I felt I could almost touch the growing fear.

Eleven

"Listen!" Richard's roar swept over the increasing babble. "We've got to get out, evacuate now!" I could hear Richard's words, but something was stopping me as if my legs had stopped working.

From a cupboard, a noise like something falling came and the door opened enough for a couple of tins of something to leap out.

Now several people screamed but did nothing. I realised that they couldn't believe the evidence of their own eyes. That shock had immobilised them.

"Get out! Everyone get out! Get into an open space away from the buildings!"

Despite my roar, only a couple of people moved, in slow motion, towards the door.

"Get out, get out!" The fire alarm sounded.

I pushed at the nearest couple of my class mates, more to clear a way for myself than for them. One or two were already out, but most were still mesmerised. More and more kids screamed.

I found myself in a mass of heaving people, struggling towards the door. My one overriding thought was to get out. Over half the class probably already had, but Mrs. Anderson still stood transfixed, as if everything was too complex for her mind to take in.

I saw Richard grab her arm and pull Then he lost his balance in the panic,

"Get out! Get out!"

I reached the door and saw Richard behind, dragging Mrs. Anderson through. A glimpse behind showed Nat still in there, pushing someone else, and I remembered she'd been one of the staggerers when the shake began.

The short corridor to the main door didn't seem damaged, but it was chaos. Kids and adults everywhere, screaming and scrabbling, desperately trying to escape the peril.

I snow ploughed my way into the crush, and was swept along and outside. The tidal wave of people flowed down the steps, separating into little pools of humans which spread like escaping water into the centre of the recreation area. The air was filled with one long, continuous scream.

For several moments I was confused, and unsure what to do now. Someone pushed me – one of the teachers. Several tutors were there already, standing like sentinels, and all shouting the same message.

"Go into your registration groups, go into your registration groups!"

"Here, over here!" Richard roared, giving Mrs. Anderson a last pull, and standing her on a garden border edging to act as a gathering point for his classmates.

I followed automatically, trying all the time to work out what was going on, and to make some kind of sense of it.

But Mrs. Anderson was beyond words, she was far too shocked. All she could say, over and over, was, "I'm sorry, I'm sorry!" in a breathless voice.

"It's all right!"

Nat staggered up, supporting a girl who was alternately screaming and crying.

"Shut up," Richard ordered. And remarkably, the girl did, at least enough for him to shout through the pandemonium, "Now, try to remember, is anyone missing? Anyone?"

The class looked round to see if all were there. I noticed Martin and Ellie and two of the loudest screamers. So far as he could tell, all my classmates were safe.

Well away from the people, a lump of masonry from the ornamental bell tower on top of the school leaned, fell, crashed against the roof, and slid slowly off. It hit the tarmac in an explosion of bits of tiles. A splash of people, still struggling out of the building from classrooms upstairs, screamed as one when a shower of dust rained on them.

Everywhere around there seemed to be a banging and a clattering. A couple of cars on the road outside looked to have bumped, panicked drivers I presumed. It could have been so much worse. The school building was still standing, it had just shaken but looked fine except for the lump of clock tower. I breathed a big sigh of relief – if this was Big Gran's warning, it was nothing. Panic over.

And then I remembered Luckry. She'd be scared, she wouldn't understand and I wouldn't be there to help her. What Mum always said, "Look after her. She's your responsibility!"

I thought I could hear the familiar voice of Big Gran in my mind. 'Now you look 'ere, young Blotch. You get to your sister and you look after 'er proper this time afore she does something daft. You 'ear?'

"Nat!" I called. "I'm going to look for Luckry! Make sure she's OK. I might take her home if I don't come back." I saw Richard nod to show he'd noticed.

Twelve

I turned to tell Mrs. Anderson the same, so that later she wouldn't think I was on the skive – Travellers have to be careful about such thoughts but she was so deeply shocked, I knew she wouldn't understand.

"I'm sorry!" she kept whispering.

I ran to the road and towards the elementary school. Everywhere, people stood about, dazed and shocked. One man leaned over his car, crying like a baby whilst another kept being sick.

The horror struck me and I broke into a run. Please God, just let her be OK, I whispered to myself. I'll never do anything nasty again, I'll become a priest, anything. Just let her be fine.

Half way there, I came across the mongrel dog. It was no longer running round and round. Instead, it sat, looking towards the junior kids' site buildings and howled. I had a terrible feeling that the dog knew something I didn't.

The mongrel loped beside me, as if it thought I had some kind of control over it all, as if I could bring the world back to a normality. I didn't shoo it I away 'cos it looked scared.

The quake must have hit the elementary school, too, but, at first, it seemed, with very little damage. "Thank God!" I sighed. I rounded the corner at a run, saw a couple of smashed tiles at the front of the building which must have shaken from the roof.

The relief as I passed the kitchens at the side and arrived on the children's' play area was enormous, for there were the kids. They were lined up, like little blue gingham or blue jumpered and grey trousered dolls: quiet, attentive, as if they'd been in a hundred quakes before. No one screaming; hardly anyone even crying; the teachers, calmly standing at the front of each line, registration books in hand, checking the names.

I stopped, several metres away from the first line.

"Thank God, Thank God!" I said to himself. "I'll never ever be nasty to Luckry again, never, I promise, I promise."

I looked along the rows of young children, understanding that they were mostly too young to have any idea of the peril they had so narrowly escaped.

My eyes searched for Luckry's fearsome teacher. Mrs. Barker was towards the far end. She was smiling and talking quietly to her line. *I can't understand why Luckry thinks she's so terrible*, I thought.

Luckry's class were all in their PE kit, with white blouses or shirts emblazoned with the school logo, black shorts or skirts, and black pumps.

There were other older kids around now, too, who'd followed me to seek their own brothers or sisters, and the elementary teachers didn't seem at all worried by their presence. Most of them they'd taught a few years before, anyway. I saw a vaguely familiar figure leaving the playground but I couldn't then remember where I'd seen him before because there was something different about him.

So where's Luckry? I must have missed her! I thought. I moved nearer Mrs. Barker's line and glanced along. A little girl, black shiny hair, thick plaits, two silver hair slides in the shape of a horse. Even when I couldn't spot her a second time, I wasn't worried. They all looked alike, in their white and black PE kit.

Mrs. Barker was calling the children's names, and they were answering, "Yes Mrs. Barker," each time. It made me feel so protective at their innocence, but above all I was just relieved.

Someone's name was being said again. Who was it? I listened, my eyes still searching for Luckry.

"Lucretia? Lucretia? Has anyone seen Lucretia?"

Something hard and heavy slammed at my back, making me stagger forward. I turned, but there was nothing there. Nothing, except an awful realisation which had struck me like falling masonry.

"Where's Luckry?" I called.

Mrs. Barker looked worried, but ignored me. "Has anyone seen Lucretia?"

"She was still getting changed in the classroom!" a little girl said.

Mrs. Richardson, the head teacher, must have guessed something was wrong. She was standing behind, now.

The teacher said, "Lucretia Morrison. She isn't here! I left her getting changed, she was so slow. I thought she was following us."

"Right!"

That was all Mrs. Richardson said. She turned, and trotted towards the building.

"Just a minute!" I called. "It's Luckry isn't it! Is she trapped? Where is she?" I didn't know why I had asked, because I knew already.

Thirteen

The anxiety pounded through me, slapping my brain into a panic.

"Luckry?" Luckry!" I shouted at the top of my voice. I knew it was pointless, because she couldn't possibly hear me.

I started to run. The speed increased, until it felt like my legs were operating on their own without the rest of me. I overtook Mrs. Richardson several metres from the entrance.

"Wait! Don't!"

I heard her shout, but nothing could stop me now – only getting Luckry out, as if she'd be standing there, waiting for me to come.

The double school doors gaped wide before me. I leaped the two steps, hearing but ignoring Mrs. Richardson's warning.

"Wait! Don't! Might be after shakes!"

The doorframe – at least, something wooden – groaned in weary shock as I passed.

Under my right foot , the floor sloped slightly oddly, and I fell. At exactly the same moment, I hit something soft that yelped. I crashed back against the wall and slumped down. There was a crack like a gun. I actually saw the doorframe snap, like a twig, and the concrete lintel slewed towards me, and fell with a mighty crash, missing me by a whisker. Part of the doorframe smashed down, and hit my leg, plaster showering in my face. Mrs Richardson was still outside.

The dog yelped once more and started howling, gazing at me, as if I was to blame.

Plaster dust made me cough and I staggered to my feet, realising that the falling wood could have done nothing worse than bruise him.

"Clumsy!" said a voice.

"Nat! But how did you get …"

"I was one step behind as you came in. Fell in!" she corrected.

"Great, thanks, have you come to help?"

"Sure, so let's just find her, and get out fast. This place looks more unsteady than our school buildings."

"Yeah, it's nasty," I agreed. "And the door's caved in, too. Let's get going, because one thing's for sure, I'm not leaving here till I've got Luckry with me. And we'll worry about how to get out again after that. The dog can look after itself."

I paused and got my bearings, remembering my own schooldays there. The school was on one level and built like a large rectangle. Down the corridor to my left the school offices and the internal entrances to the kitchen. Ahead, the massive hall used for PE and for lunch, down one side of which ran the kitchens. To my right, a corridor with classrooms on either side, with more at the far side of the hall.

I turned to the right down the corridor. At first, apart from a few bits of plaster and the occasional book on the floor, it looked normal. But a second look showed the truth – everywhere lay evidence of the quake because of a hurried departure. A child's shoe, an opened and abandoned snack box, some pencils and books, a paint smeared apron, several small toys.

I was aware that the dog was beside me. The howl had become a sort of whine, in which it opened and shut its mouth.

"Go away, stupid dog. I've enough on with Luckry. You'll have to save yourself."

From behind, Nat shouted, "Hang on, think it out! Don't just go anywhere!"

I shouted Luckry's name.

I stopped, and strained my ears. The dog's yammering made it difficult to hear if Luckry called back, but I thought I'd heard something.

"Shut up you stupid dog." Nat caught me up. "Wait, listen, she can't …"

"Quiet! And you!" I picked up a piece of plaster and threw it at the dog, not to hurt it, but to drive it away, so I could hear better because there was something else, a noise not part of our's, or the dog's. It almost sounded like a child, talking to itself.

The plaster hit the dog, which stopped howling immediately. The plaster bounced onto the floor and the dog ran to it, picked it up, and ran back to me with it, dropped it, and started howling again.

"Great!" said Nat. "Playing catch now."

"You stupid dog!" I snarled and kicked out at it. "Luckry!" I shouted again, as the dog's howling broke its rhythm. "Did you hear something, Nat?"

She didn't need to reply, because there was definitely someone there. Someone quite close, I reckoned. Definitely a child. I could hear a voice!

"In here!" I shouted. I was beside the third classroom, and knew the voice was from there.

"No wait!" Nat called again.

"Thank God!" I replied. "She's in here. Not half as hard as I feared. Luckry! It's Blotch, big brother."

The classroom door opened easily. I could hear the child's voice clearly now, calm, as if it was describing something.

Books lay scattered on the floor. A couple of chairs had been overturned. It was eerie, like an abandoned ship. The voice was quite loud in here, but, oddly, it wasn't calling for help.

It was a voice of someone reading a story.

A pc flashed pictures at the back of the room suddenly stopped and automatically started again.

The child's voice stopped and re-started with it.

"I tried to tell you," Nat sighed. "This is the aural work room."

The dog howled again in sympathy.

Fourteen

"You stupid fool!"

I couldn't help myself – I roared the words across the room. They cut the silence like a broadsword, I was so bubbling with rage at my own stupidity. "Wasting time! As if she really could be in here when it isn't even her classroom!"

"Calm down Blotch and don't panic. That's what I was trying to say. If we try and check every room, we'll just waste time. Think it through. We've got to go for the places she might be."

I knew she was right; I kicked out at one of the tables in frustration, and regretted it with the pain.

"You're right. It's no good standing here," I replied as normally as rage would let me. "Come on, she was doing PE, so she'll be in the hall."

I turned back towards the hall with Nat immediately behind and was just in time to see the dog's tail disappearing somewhere out of the room.

"Well, at least I scared that stupid thing away," I muttered. "Or perhaps ..." I hesitated at the implication of the thought. "Perhaps it knows something we don't. Like an aftershock on its way."

"Exactly!" Nat agreed.

I laughed at my own foolishness. "Course not! It's so thick it wouldn't even know itself."

My chuckle aimed at reassuring me, but it didn't.

The hall fire door was shut, but pushed open easily.

From down the offices' corridor, I heard the headteacher's voice calling, "Lucretia! Tom, Natalie, Lucretia!"

It panicked me into thrusting myself through the doorway.

"Wow!" Nat gasped. "It's like something out of a horror movie!"

At this end of the hall, everything was eerily expectant. PE hoops, skittles and beanbags were spattered on the floor. But at the far end, a quick glance showed that a chunk of plaster had cascaded onto the floor and imploded and lay in half-demolished chunks. A thin layer of plaster dust lay over everything like icing sugar. Occasionally, it made us both cough.

Or was it the smell of escaping gas? The smell wasn't unbearable, but it was there, and it probably showed that, somewhere, perhaps in the kitchens which ran alongside the hall, a pipe had ruptured.

The hatchway into the kitchen, through which meals were served, was shut, but I thought she couldn't have gone there. Nat was already charging about, glancing behind curtains and larger PE apparatus. My less organized search was interrupted by a banging against the hatchway.

"Luckry?"

I remembered something I'd read. In a fire, young children try to hide from the danger. They get into cupboards or hide under tables – just what Luckry would do!

"She's in there!" I shouted. "Luckry!"

There was another thump on the hatchway, as if she'd heard and was agreeing.

I pushed up the hatchway cover easily and stared inside.

"I'm not convinced," said Nat. "Oh!"

The thumper was immediately obvious: A disorientated, terrified and probably half-gassed bird flew jerkily round the kitchens, now and then banging into things.

I looked down the row of stainless steel ovens and warmers, pot cupboards and sterilisers. "Even so, we ought to check."

I scrambled onto the hatchway top and dropped with ease into the kitchen.

"Hell, gas!" Nat cried, easily jumping through after me.

The smell was much stronger here. I picked up a cloth for wiping dishes, held it over my mouth to help me breathe and threw a second to Nat.

"You're supposed to ventilate the room," I announced. "I read it somewhere and where's it turn off?" I opened the outer door of the kitchen, looked out but saw no one.

"Where are the rescuers?

Nat was already searching the kitchen. Near the hatchways, the thought of gas and electricity and who knew what other dangers almost made me consider giving up the search, but only for a brief moment. Surely, the rescuers would be here soon.

Or would they? If half the town had been hit, disastrously they might not come for hours.

"Luckry! Luckry!"

With the gas clearer now, I stuffed the tea towel into my pocket and started searching from the other end of the stainless steel cabinets, calling Luckry's name at each one.

I was nearly getting to Nat's search end when Nat stopped suddenly. I looked to see why.

"Oh my God!" she said.

A foot poked out between two rows.

"It can't be Luckry," I sighed.

"I know that!" Nat snapped. "Thing is – oh heck – we can't just stand here! Come on!" She reached out and touched the ankle. "It's still warm."

Fifteen

I hesitated. Entering the 'quake-hit building was easier than this. I hadn't been thinking straight then ut the notion that there could be a body lying there beside the ovens scared me to death because we Romanies have a thing about ghosts and dead people.

What if the gas built up, too? Then I heard – the gas was hissing next to me and I glimpsed round, terrified at the idea of an explosion, and saw the cause. A gas ring on a cooker was on, but not lit. I turned it off.

"I found the gas problem," I announced.

Nat crouched beside the person. "Great!" she said. "Now solve this. It's a woman, she's hurt, and she needs help."

She was on her back and it was obviously one of the cooks, her white overall shining with cleanliness. I crouched down beside her, next to a large aluminium pan. Nearby, a mass of peeled potatoes were strewn over the floor. I felt her neck pulse. "She's alive!"

"I just told you that. We've got to help her."

"I know!" I snapped back, but I could have wept at the frustration, because I knew she had to have priority even before the search for Luckry. We did this first aid course on our site as people are forever getting hurt living in unsafe environments like sites can be or the sort of work we often do such as scrap metal or cutting trees so I had some idea what to do. I knelt beside her chest, turned her face towards me, and pulled her jaw down to make sure she could breathe well. I could find no obviously broken bones. I put her arm along her side and lifted her far leg, so the knee was up in the air. The far arm went over her chest, then I pulled. She slid, easily, into a good position to recover.

I saw her head. "Look!" I pointed. "It must have been the pan. Maybe she was kneeling, and the pan fell on her."

A large patch of blood on her head seemed to confirm the theory.

"She's coming round," Nat announced.

Sure enough, the cook groaned and moved slightly.

"Listen! Can you hear me?" I asked. I wasn't sure if she could or not.

"I'm trying to find my sister, have you seen her at all? Lucretia Morrison?"

I bent my head to listen in case she spoke, but she didn't.

Nat muttered irritatedly. "As if she would."

"We've got to go and look for Luckry," I explained, unsure how much the woman could understand. "But we can't leave you here. It isn't safe. There could be afterquakes, and you could get trapped. Somehow, we've got to get you out of the building."

"How?" Nat asked. "That head injury looks bad and dragging her across the floor'll just make her worse."

"We'll shout for help." I ran to the outside door and looked out. I felt as though the entire world was somewhere else. Still not a person in sight, and the playground where the children and teachers had assembled was at the back of the building.

"Help!" I tried. "Help!" louder.

No one. Not even the stupid dog.

I went back to the woman who was still in exactly the position, but breathing normally. Nat kept stroking her hair and talking soothingly to her.

"Now what?" Nat asked.

I ignored her. "Listen!" I tried again with the cook. "We're going to have to try and drag you out."

"Great! Oh great! Kill her while we're at it, why don't we?"

I tucked my arms under her armpits, and tried to pull. She seemed an incredible weight, and when I half lifted her shoulders, her head flopped down. "Help me!"

My frustration felt it would explode. I thought of Luckry, caught somewhere, terrified at what had happened, too frightened to do anything. The woman was holding up the search by seeming to be a colossal weight, more than I could ever have imagined. "Help me, Nat," I gasped again.

Nat sighed and did nothing. *"We* need help," she said.

"But, Nat, I've looked, and there isn't any. None! The emergency services aren't here yet, and who knows when they'll come. They could all be trapped themselves for all I know."

Nat just sighed again, walked across the kitchen, and moments later came back pushing a large stainless steel trolley with big rubber wheels. It had two shelves, the lower being very low, as if to move large and heavy drums of food.

Getting her onto the low shelf wasn't easy, and took several attempts. Eventually, I jammed the trolley against some ovens so it wouldn't move, and between us we lifted her shoulders and head, little by little, as carefully as we could, easing the top half of her body onto it. A smear of blood showed the head wound was still oozing. Finally, only half her legs wouldn't fit. I made her as comfortable as I could, turning her head to let the air into her lungs. Then, gently, slowly – but never forgetting Luckry for a second – I pulled her to the outside door, as Nat carried the legs.

The trapped bird found the door at the same time and shot out.

"Round to the playground," I shouted. There, most of the children still stood in lines, noisier now, with more crying and more babbling of excited talk. I realised, with a shock, that only a few minutes had passed since we first went into the school. More adults were about – probably motorists from the abandoned cars, and a sprinkling of parents, too, trying to organize the children.

"Hey!" I shouted, and when a teacher looked my way, pointed to the cook on the trolley. "She needs help!" I explained.

Before anyone could speak further, Nat and I turned and ran back into the kitchen, heading for the hall.

Sixteen

I imagined the teacher's calmness when the quake struck. Only the teachers would understand what was happening. I imagined Mrs. Barker's words: *'Everyone put down what you're holding and line up at the door ... Right, off we go outside'* – then a line of small children marching out of a danger they couldn't comprehend.

"Luckry!" I whispered fearfully.

I saw Nat disappear into a PE store to search.

Half way along the hall wall, opposite a bank of largely intact windows, a clock ticked away the missing lesson. It was exactly ten minutes past ten o'clock.

"Luckry!"

I could hear the head teacher shouting my sister's name as well. Her voice was softer and more distant, with a tang of fear, but it brought me back to reality.

Where were the rescue services? If only they'd hurry, but I'd already worked out the answer. If the quake had been even worse elsewhere in the town, the rescuers would already be heavily involved and rescuers from other areas would still be on the way.

I picked my way across the floor, stepping over nothing worse than the apparatus of the lesson. In the middle of the hall, a PE rope hung forlornly.

But at the far end of the hall, things were very different. Something massive – it could have been a roof beam – had poked itself into the hall like a finger through pie crust. Beside it, a strip light spun lazily from its wire. Rubble from the holed wall, mainly plaster, had crashed down, onto and over the piano.

The stool made me think of Luckry, sitting on it, trying to unknot and fasten her accursed laces. And suddenly ...

"Luckry?" I whispered. My voice couldn't say the name loudly because of the dust-laden sobs that hung in my throat, refusing to let me concentrate.

"Luckry?"

A little stronger, and with that strength I threw himself onto the floor and began scrabbling at the rubble which piled against the wall, and over the piano. You could see most of the top of it but couldn't actually see the piano stool. I knew there was one because I remembered it from my own time in the school. It had been brown wood with a leather seat and round handles which you turned to make the seat go higher or lower.

"Luckry? Luckry? It's Blotch. There was no reply, but I was certain she was there. "Nat! She's under here."

It wasn't possible to tell which was solid rubble and which loose bits because of the layer of dust disguising everything, but as my hands clawed into the pile, my fingers caught against hidden sharp edges. I ignored the pain.

I tugged and pulled, heaving away large lumps of plaster, throwing shards of plaster laden timber strips behind.

"Luckry? Can you hear? Are you there?"

But the reply I so longed for did not come.

I resolved that, if I found her, safe, I'd buy her some new pumps out of my own money – elastic ones, which didn't need laces. She'd never go through this again. Never!

Seventeen

I paused to cough. Somewhere near me, rubble moved. I started, expecting to have to leap away from a fall. For a split second I was convinced there'd been another after quake, till I saw, barely a metre away, Nat, digging like mad with her own bare hands.

"Nat! Thanks!" I panted.

"Just dig," she said. "And shut up! Listen for her."

Her digging was more frenzied than mine, and when I looked at my hands I realised why. The pain from the worn skin, cuts and early blisters, which I hadn't noticed till now, slowed me down.

I pulled at a large lump of plaster and dragged it to one side. In front, a small hole appeared, just big enough for a hand to get in. My fingertips touched into the hole, and I tried to work out what was in it. It was like one of those learning games from your first school, when you put your hand in a box, touch something, and have to work out what it is.

What I now touched wasn't flesh. It felt hard and smooth, but not cold. "Wood! The piano stool leg."

I groped to make the hole wider and longer. Now I could get my arm in up to the elbow, then nearly to my shoulder.

There was something metallic, smooth, which felt like the end of a golf club – which it couldn't be. And when I pressed, the piano's skeleton gave a dull music-less thud.

"The piano pedal. Nothing there!" Disappointment gripped me. I'd imagined that finding her would be quick and easy.

To be sure, I felt more to each side of the little hole, and was about to finally take my arm out when one finger touched something slightly rubbery. I dug away further round it, and yanked it out.

"Oh!"

The shock of the find made me cry out.

"What?" asked Nat. "Have you found her?"

I held out the PE pump for her to see.

"Bad luck," she said, and kept digging.

"What do you mean? It could be Luckry's!"

"It's double tied. Properly, like an adult would. And anyway it's too small for hers. But you'd better keep digging in case. There could be another child there."

I dug on, but somehow my heart wasn't in it. Now, I was increasingly convinced she couldn't be there. The piano stool must be still standing, and if she'd been on it when the rubble hit her, she'd have been squashed down next to the piano, and she wasn't there. I couldn't think this pump belong to any trapped child, either. It had come away far too easily to be wedged onto someone's foot.

A groan somewhere behind made me stop digging. I knew the sound now. Part of the building was giving up the fight to stay standing. I turned in time to see a large chunk of ceiling fall, and crash onto the floor behind. It bounced once towards Nat, smashed like pottery, and a cloud of dust rose, hesitated, and spread. Automatically, I put my hands over my head, glancing up to see if another lump was about to fall down, but it still looked secure.

"This building's unsafe," I announced to Nat as she knocked and shook dust from her hair.

The sarcasm dripped. "Really?" She knelt in the midst of a sea of rubble which she'd torn from in front, and had spread into my end.

"Look," she said. "Luckry's not here. She can't be or we'd have found her by now. You've got to face it Blotch, she isn't here. Every minute we spend in this building makes us likely to be the *next* ones to be trapped. We've done all we can."

She stood. "Come on, let's get out before we're killed," she pleaded.

I stood reluctantly, turning with a sense of heart-torn failure and started following Nat towards the hall door where we'd come in, picking my way past the newly rubble strewn floor.

I've failed, I thought. *I was grumpy 'cos of having to walk her to school, and now I haven't even got a sister.*

Face it, she's dead. If only I'd helped her with her PE pumps, she'd have been out now and safe with the other kids. Those wretched PE pumps. I imagined her again, putting them on and trying to undo the stupid knots. But we could go no further. A new pile of ceiling rubble from the fall when we'd been searching at the opposite end stopped us. The door in or out of the hall was now effectively blocked.

"Through the kitchen," I ordered, then saw Nat was already on the serving counter and about to drop through.

At that moment, I realised. We'd been looking in the wrong place. Luckry wouldn't have been changing in the hall, anyway. This wasn't a secondary school with its own changing rooms. They got changed in a classroom! A child outside had even said that, but I'd been too shocked then to take it in. Yes, that'd be where she was. I'd been looking in the wrong place!

"Wait!" I said. "Luckry – I know where she is!"

Eighteen

You don't expect earthquakes in Britain, do you? I know now that they do happen, though. Sure they're not usually very big at all and the worst thing that can happen seems to be a chimney falling down and on the Richter scale they never get above about 4 or 5 at the very worst.

When they first wanted to do fracking in our area, most people living round here went ballistic. There were protests and petitions, marches, sit ins at the entrance to the proposed site and some nasty scenes of people getting even more worked up than if it had been a proposed to put a Traveller site there. Nobody from our caravan site went to the protests. There'd been a little earthquake in Blackpool a few years ago but the firm said they'd learned what went wrong there and it couldn't happen again. I'm not saying it was the fracking caused this one at all, but I reckon it was a combination of things – the dumping of the chemicals deep underground at Marshall Meadows, the weight and pressure of Devil's Hole reservoir and the actual fracking at Tibbs Thorns Farm. That's the theory we have here on the site and I've seen it suggested in the local paper, too.

Imagine a thin trapezium shape. On the bottom line to the right is where our site is. To the left it's Marshall Meadows. The side at right angles to the site is Devil's Hole Reservoir about two miles North and to the North East of that, due north from Marshall Meadows, is Tibbs Thorn Farm which is where they began fracking.

When there was a public meeting, Dad went to represent the site residents. Actually, nobody on the site was against it because Romani people end up on the worst bits of land next to sewage works and on flood plains so fracking a few miles away didn't bother us in the slightest. It couldn't make things worse – on the site, we hoped some people might even be able to get non-skilled jobs there labouring because everyone wants to work and being a Traveller can make it difficult to find. As soon as you put 'Marshall Meadows Traveller Site' on an application, the companies suddenly find lots of better people for the job or there was no vacancy in the first place. So many lies have been printed about us in the past that people think we're all thieves and violent and dirty. Actually, amongst my relatives I don't know anyone who's any of those things.

At school, we did a special project on fracking so I knew a bit about it. They were after natural gas – hydraulic fracturing is what they call it really. Natural gas is much less harmful to the atmosphere than a lot of other things – we use a lot of propane on the site and we even thought there may have been a way for us to get cheaper gas for ourselves instead, direct from the fracking site. A stupid dream, of course.

Anyway, what they do is drill down and deep underground they pump in a mix of water, sand and chemicals. That stuff fractures the shale rocks and making cracks bigger so the trapped gas can seep out and up the surface. Trouble is, there are fears that some of the chemicals they use could be harmful, especially as a lot of it comes back to the surface and it can then be contaminated with dangerous additional chemicals such as heavy metals. The other problem is that the sand and what not can act like a kind of oil and make the huge rocks deep underground more likely to slide or move just a bit because friction is reduced – and then you get a tiny earthquake.

Just like the one we'd just had, with Luckry trapped somewhere because of it, so it was that which drove me on.

Nineteen

"Thomas, you're in huge danger," said a voice. I swung round at the same time as Nat dropped down from the hatchway back into the kitchen and so did I. I hadn't noticed Mrs. Richardson there, and crashed straight into her.

"Sorry! I didn't see you. But Lucretia – I know where she is."

Nat stood beside me.

Mrs. Richardson held my shoulders gently. "I came to tell you to get out, quickly. The whole building is unsafe – they say parts were jerry built. The only way out now is through the kitchen. Everywhere else is blocked off. But she can't be in here ..."

"I know, she's in the classroom," I interrupted.

"That way's blocked too, and very dangerous. I've checked and I can't get through from the outside either. Let the experts rescue Lucretia – they're arriving now."

"She's right – we've done all we can." Nat grabbed my shirt and pulled gently towards the outside door. "Let's get out. Leave it to the professionals."

I shook her off, at the same time noticing Mrs. Richardson's face. A big smudge of dirt ran down one cheek, otherwise she looked as well-groomed as ever – like a business woman on her way to a convention. Her very smartness irritated me even more than the fact that she wasn't willing to keep searching.

"I have to find Luckry," I explained, slamming out each word.

"Please, Tom," said Mrs. Richardson. "You don't understand the danger. You could be killed at any moment. The whole building might be unsafe. It's obvious that there were flaws in the construction of the school – cheap materials."

"I understand this, Mrs. Richardson. It's my little sister trapped somewhere here and I'm the only one who seems to want to get her out!"

I used the words to hurl out some of my own anger and hurt someone else. I knew they were untrue. It wasn't that no one wanted to get her out, but that no one here yet could. "Just because she couldn't do her pumps, no one bothered about her. Well I do!" I insisted.

Mrs. Richardson shook her head. "That's not true, Tom. Every other child in the school was evacuated successfully. Even all the adults are accounted for now thanks to your finding Mrs. Waters. We'd realised she was unaccounted for and the fire service were about to search for her, too. But this isn't the place to talk. Please, let's get you and Nat out now."

At that moment, the hall walls groaned again and two windows cracked. I ducked automatically.

"Quickly! Please, Tom! It won't help anyone for you to be trapped here, too!"

Gently, I pushed Mrs. Richardson's hands from my shoulders. "I'm sorry. I know, I know all that you said is true really. But I have to. Luckry's my kid sister, see, and in a kind of way it was all my fault."

Somewhere outside, an emergency vehicle's siren came gradually nearer.

"Your fault?" Mrs. Richardson made a grab at my arm but missed. "Tom! Wait! Please! We've got to make you safe – Lucretia wouldn't want a dead or injured brother. Come on!"

I was about to leap back through the hatchway when someone grabbed my foot and yanked. Then two more hands grabbed my arms, not savagely but so I couldn't move. I turned and was face to face with a big fireman, and with Nat holding my leg. Nat gave me one of her slaps, friendly but determined. "Out!" she said. She let go and the fireman turned me towards the door.

I felt Nat shove me in the back then I was outside and hundreds of cameras were flashing into my eyes and people were shouting, "Hey, Terrific Two, Tell us how you rescued Mrs. Waters. You'll get a medal for this." I was dazed and couldn't have answered even if I'd wanted to.

Twenty

It looked very different now in the schoolyard. There were lots more people, and an ambulance, police cars and several fire engines. The firemen were obviously going in and out of the building and it looked like there was a lot of activity at the far end, which is the bit of the school above the cellars and the boiler. I'd been down there once with the caretaker when I was a pupil to fetch a ball which had somehow got there.

A policeman took me by the arm and led the three of us round from the back of the building where we had come from the kitchen, round the side of the building and past the dustbins to the back of the building and the main playground which was also where the normal entrances to the school were. I realised then that the press people weren't in the yard as I'd thought for their photos but hanging over the school wall at the front of the building, at the road side.

On the third side of the building masses of people stood at the far end of the yard behind a 'do not cross' police barrier. There were hardly any children now – parents must have come to collect them. I saw one or two people I knew from the site, not there for kids but support for we Morrisons and I suppose curiosity, but there was no chance to speak to them. The policeman swept us on to a small white caravan parked actually in the main part of the playground. On the side it said, 'Police. Family Liaison'.

A woman came to the door. "Come in, please. I'm Karen Whitesmith," she said, as we went in. "I'm the family liaison for your family, Tom."

I looked past her and saw Mum sitting with Dad. Dad looked drawn and worried. Mum had been crying and her face was even blotchier than mine. I pushed past Karen and threw my arms round Mum. "I'm sorry Mum. I couldn't find her. It's all my fault and the emergency people didn't come."

My face was wet – I wasn't sure if it was my tears or Mum's.

"There were big accidents on two of the main roads in town and one on the bypass – people panicking at the quake," Karen explained. "We were all very delayed."

"Anyway, it's not your fault, son," said Dad. "It was an earthquake. Vaffedi bok, that's all."

Oh, that means bad luck – it's what we say a lot – vaffedi or vasavao bok for bad and kushti bok for good luck.

But, you see, it was my fault and I hadn't been able to put it right. Now she was probably lying dead under rubble. I'd been horrid to her and I hadn't helped her about the laces. If I had – if I had – she'd have been able to leave the building with the rest of her class.

I blurted all this out to Dad and the police lady. There was no sign of Mrs. Richardson but Nat was still hovering in the doorway. I saw Karen nod and mouth some words to a police officer behind Nat.

Karen led me to a seat by Mum. "Let me explain," Karen said. "You've got it wrong. The earthquake was very minor and there were no reports of damage anywhere except the bit at your school and at Lucretia's. I think parts of your sister's school building were jerry built – it's something we're looking into – so they were weaker than they should have been but in fact there wasn't much damage in the school, it just looked worse, and we doubt if Lucretia could be buried under rubble. But we're making sure right now. She's more likely to have hidden herself in a cupboard somewhere to escape danger. So don't worry, because we're sure we'll find her."

I noticed that she didn't say if she meant find her alive or dead but I said nothing. "There are loads of firemen in the building," she continued, "searching absolutely everywhere, every cupboard and cubby hole, behind every piece of furniture – all the places a terrified six year old might hide. If she is there, we'll find her, but if she isn't there …" The unfinished words hung over all our heads, like a sword waiting to slash down.

Twenty One

"So you see ," Dad said at last. "It wasn't your fault at all – just vaffedi bok. We thought we'd lost you as well, going in that building like that. Worrying about one is bad enough – why, did you think you were, a Ninja?"

I tried to grin but the lump in my throat stopped me. "No," was all I could manage.

"Er, I think I'd better be going," said Nat from the doorway.

"Please, no Natalie, I think it would be good if you stayed," said Karen, "you being Tom's pal, you see. We've already told your own parents that you're safe and that you're fine so they won't worry."

Nat nodded and sat down at the far end. I didn't understand why I might need a friend really, unless the news was terrible and then I'd just want my mum and dad.

Karen said they couldn't get into the cellar because the way down was blocked – it's actually got a separate outdoor entrance so I don't know why that was the case but I thought it doubtful that Luckry could be there. "We are a little worried still as so far there's no sign of her and we presume she was the last to leave the building, but the head teacher searched everywhere before she came out and saw no children."

Just then, a policeman stuck his head in the doorway and beckoned Karen over and I knew the news was bad.

After a muttered conversation, Karen came up to us, looking grave. "Look," she said, "we don't know what to make of this but we've found two things – this PE pump is one and we think it's hers."

She held it out. Mum gave a shriek – it was Luckry's for sure; small, black, laces in a huge knot and the clincher was the name on the inside of the tongue, written by Mum in a red marker, 'Lucretia M'.

"Where was it?" Dad's voice was shaky and his eyes were watery.

"It was in her classroom, Mr. Morrison, near a wall."

"I knew she was in there ," I interrupted. "That's where I wanted to go next to search, but nobody would let me. I could have found her by now, but would anyone …"

"No, she certainly isn't there. I have to stress that there was very little damage at all in there, but there was no actual sign of her except that the window was open, and outside it, underneath, we found the second thing, this little shoe as well."

Mum wailed again. She took it from Karen and pushed the blue plastic side to reveal 'LM'. "There may be a very simple explanation for it all, but it is odd to say the least," Karen went on. "We need your help to fit in some of the missing pieces so, Tom, did anything unusual happen on the way to school?"

I explained about the whole sorry journey and I left nothing out about me being nasty and impatient and Nat added other bits when I forgot them. I'd got all the way through to the wishing well bit when Mum gave another shriek.

"The money!"

"Yes, I know. I think it was a £2 she chucked in the stupid old well, but she'd thrown it before I even realised. I know it was too much to put in. I'd got a penny in my pocket to give her – but I was too late and she said it was for a big wish. Maybe we could get it back."

Mum shook her head vehemently. "It wasn't an everyday £2 coin – she'd opened her money pig and the coin she took was Big Gran's Golden Jubilee coin, but she'd also taken a ten-pound note and a five pound one. We found it when we got back with the vehicle parts Dad wanted. Why did she need all that?"

I didn't understand. I was sure she couldn't have thrown two notes in or I'd have seen. But the gold coin was much more serious. Big Gran Lucretia had left an 1887 Queen Victoria gold £5 Jubilee coin to each of her grandchildren – eleven children including Luckry and me. There was a twelfth coin which she gave to Mum and Dad. They'd lost my baby sister Ruby the same day she was born, but Big Gran gave them the coin in case Mum and Dad had another but so far they haven't.

"I didn't know it was Big Gran's coin!" I protested. "She was always saying that Big Gran tells her to do things," I added, "and Big Gran told her to throw in a big coin for a big wish, but I thought it was just an everyday £2 coin. Well, that's what she said." I really couldn't get my head round it – *all that money and above all the valuable coin for a really big wish?*

"OK," said Karen. "This little girl, only six years old, disappears in an earthquake. Not a bad one, but it must have been very frightening for someone so young. The rest of her class had already gone to the hall for the PE lesson when it struck. So why didn't she just follow them to the hall? Because she only had one PE pump on," – (my heart sank under another wave of guilt) – "so she wasn't ready. We've found her clothes at her table in the classroom so she'd changed into her PE shorts and singlet over her undies. The little earthquake must have panicked her yet she goes out of the window to escape it. Why and where is she now?" Another wail from Mum. "We suspect she wandered off, perhaps trying to get back home or find her brother, so I imagine she's wandering around somewhere but we can't be sure. I should say, without alarming you, that it's unlikely she's been snatched – there's no evidence for it – though we can't rule it out, but there are lots of other dangers around."

Twenty Two

Mum was really crying now and Dad had his arm round her and was hugging her for all he was worth. I would have been crying but I deliberately didn't look at Mum and kept swallowing it down so seeing my tears didn't make Mum even more upset.

"Of course we're already searching now, but we're bringing in lots more officers from other areas and we'll be appealing for people in the area to keep their eyes open and report anything," Karen added. "I hope she's found quickly – it's early days yet – but if not we shall ask for volunteers searching, too."

"Snatched?" Dad whispered the word. "Kidnapped? By one of those, those ..."

"There may be a simpler and more innocent explanation." Karen tapped Dad on his arm to comfort him. "We're doing all we can. We're in the process of collecting CCTV from all over, but so far nothing."

"I must go and search." Dad pulled himself free from Mum, but Karen held out her arm to stop him.

"No, you must stay here with me. I know you want to help but it's important we have you here to answer any questions we may have in the hunt to find her. What I really don't understand is taking the money – it's a puzzle because she obviously needed the notes to buy something or to spend to get somewhere. That suggests she had another plan. I wonder, was there anything worrying her? Have you got any clues?"

We all shook our heads. The only worry I could think of was the PE pumps and I'd made that worse. I saw Nat look intently at me, saw her read my mind. She stood,"Fifteen pounds would buy a good pair of flip-flop slip on pumps," she said. I blurted out in more detail about her worries over the laces and the knots.

"Right." Karen got on her radio. There were only three or four places in town where she might have got them, but then, being only six it raised the question as to whether she'd even go to the obvious place or to some cut price bargain shop or somewhere ludicrous in her hunt for some – if she'd gone at all.

"I could go," said Nat. "I could check anywhere that might sell them. It'll save police time while you search for her."

"No," Karen shook her head. "In any case, I want both you, Mr. and Mrs Morrison and you Tom and you Nat to go back to the site now and wait there. I'm going to arrange to bring this family liaison caravan over here as well. I'll act as your police liaison of course, so you don't need to worry about putting me up because I'll stay 'til we find her and I can sleep in this, so I think it would be a good idea for Nat to come for the time being, too. A good friend is what Tom needs at the moment, but as to Lucretia, could she … could she have run away from home for some other reason?" We all shook our heads violently. "Is there someone she's very fond of and would like to go and stay with, a school friend or a relative maybe?"

"We're a tight family." Mum wiped an eye with the back of her hand. "She's got a couple of good friends at school and she's been at sleep-overs at their houses and they've been to us, too, but she'd have seen them at school today anyway I expect." Karen made a note of their names to check. It didn't seem very likely to me.

"OK," Karen smiled, "I'm going to get you taken home in a police car. I'll follow with this caravan and perhaps you can find somewhere near your trailer where I can park up to stay. Nat, you can go with Tom and his family."

"My van's on the road," Dad said. "So I'll have to drive that."

Karen shook her head. "No, when you're worried like you are, it's asking for an accident to happen. A police colleague will bring it for you, but try not to worry. We're doing all we can."

Twenty Three

Travellers who I'd seen looking on at the school earlier had drifted in ones and twos back to the site and they watched respectfully at a distance as we climbed out of the police car and went into our trailer. You'd have thought I'd still remember riding in a police car to this day, but I don't, my mind was too screwed to remember anything but Luckry.

"Come in, Nat," Mum said.

Karen and her caravan turned up a few moments later towed by a police Range Rover, then the copper who brought Dad's van. Courtesy's very important on a Traveller site and any visitors are normally plied with mugs of tea and food within moments, but not today – you could see Mum was far too uptight about Luckry to be thinking about such things. We left Karen doing the basic setting up of her caravan where she was going to stay as our family liaison and we four, I mean including Nat, huddled together in our trailer.

Granny Rayni arrived a few moments after to do the usual site thing. She had a tray of steaming mugs of very sweet tea on a tray, served in posh mugs as if we were the visitors.

"Here," she said handing them round. "This'll make you feel a bit better – the cup that cheers," and realised her mistake. "Usually," she added, screwing her face against the inappropriateness of the remark. "Oh and by the way, it's been on the local TV news as a flash. They had a picture of her in her school uniform," (I guessed an official school photo) "and said she was missing after the little 'quake and would anyone who thought they'd seen her ring the incident room number." Mum's hand shook as she tried to sip from the tea mug.

Dad nodded, though how much he'd really taken in I don't know. "They'll be checking the paedos I expect ," he said, and swallowed hard. I heard Mum give an involuntary sob. The tea was very sweet and milky and I couldn't drink mine for thinking about Luckry.

Karen knocked on the door and Granny Rayni ushered her in. I guessed Granny Rayni would act as door guard now because if you want a good guard, she's the Rottweiler. That's another Romani thing – if you have a problem, people always rally round and in the past they'd even feed people in hard times for weeks for no pay-back. Karen gave Granny Rayni a glance as if to ask who she was, but Granny told her before she could say anything and it brooked no suggestion that she should leave.

Karen sat down. "An update," she said. "I've got the caravan set up for me and we're plugging it direct into the site electricity supply in the power fuse box. Don't worry about the extra cost of the electric, we'll sort it all out later."

Dad shook his head. "I'm not bothered – I just want my little angel back."

"Yes," added Karen, "as regards that, we've got teams of police fanning out from the school, searching and doing house to house moving out from the school. Some are searching towards town in case she went that way, others towards the secondary school and to the industrial estate and to the start of Marshall Meadows in case she's trying to walk back home. We've a team going through the school grounds with a fine tooth comb. We've got officers at the bus station, too, everyone looking for a little girl and showing pictures of her and asking for information. Local TV news has had it on – there have been several responses and we're checking them all out now. We've got no definite sightings yet but it's hardly twelve noon so we're on to it very quickly."

"What about the paedos?" Dad asked. "Have you thought of them?"

Karen nodded. "Detectives are going to the addresses of all molesters right now, but there's absolutely nothing to suggest that. At the moment we're working on the theory that she was scared in the quake, panicked, and got out through the classroom window."

Someone brought a big plate of ham sandwiches to the door and Granny Raini took them and began offering them round to us all on some of our fancy guest plates. I didn't want anything but Nat munched a couple. We're big eaters of pig meat but there are some things we will never touch. Nat had just taken an extra-large bite when Karen's police phone rang. I heard Karen saying things like, "Yes, I see, oh," and I guessed something was wrong.

She looked grave. "Has she ever been to a café called the 'World's End'? Does she know anybody there?"

I think my heart stopped beating at the moment and Nat began to choke on her sandwich.

Twenty Four

Karen tried to sound reassuring but it didn't work.

Mum shook her head. "We do use cafés but we're a bit particular – hygiene and things – it's important to all Travellers how food's prepared and served, like Muslims with halal meat and Jews, only we have different ones. So there are only a couple of cafés we use in the big stores and never 'World's End', you see, it's a bit, sort of, scruffy there."

I wondered what Karen would think about Travellers suggesting somewhere was not good enough for them – people think of us as being dirty and scruffy and the lowest of the low and they see our sites next to the worst pieces of land where no-one else would live. Some sites are disgusting and let us all down, I admit that, but Dad won't stand for that on ours. Yet sometimes if we go to see non-Travellers, Mum and Dad will politely say no to coffee or tea because they're worried the china will be, sort of, polluted. I don't mean dirty, it's much more than that and we even think some animals are unclean. Sorry, yes, I'm going off the story – where was I? Oh yes.

Strangely, outside I thought I could hear a sort of hum, like a swarm of bees or a bumble bee nest but it was a bit later I found what it was because at that point Karen explained, "There's a man uses the café a lot and we've had worries about him. He was seen hanging about Lucretia's school after the 'quake."

I felt like I'd been smacked on the head because I realised exactly who she meant so that both Nat and I tried to tell Karen at the same time. Nat won. She explained how we'd seen a man with billboards advertising the café on the way to school and the conversation and the finger off sign he gave. I hadn't exactly heard what he'd shouted, but Nat had: 'You want to take better care of that little girl and stop dragging her around. One day, she might get lost.' I think my heart stopped again.

"And I saw him at Luckry's school just before I went in the building," I added. "You don't think ...?"

Karen said, "We just have to check it out."

"He was near the well – could he have thrown her down it?" I asked in panic.

"The searchers have already been to the well and the padlock's on tight on the top, but I'm going to pass on what you've just told me about the man and what he said," and she nipped out of the trailer and I heard her talking on her phone, though I couldn't hear the words.

"I know what he looks like," I said as she came back in. "Can Nat and I go and look for him? Have you checked the café?"

Karen shook her head. "He's not there. It may mean nothing but we need to check further. Certainly Lucretia's

94

not at the café because although we didn't have a search warrant, the owner very willingly let us look all over the building for her in case she was hidden there but the man doesn't live there anyway."

"What sort of, I mean, what's this man done – in the past I mean?" Nat asked.

"I'm not allowed to tell you that except that he has never been to gaol." She glanced at Nat and I: "Why don't you two go for a walk round the site and get a breath of fresh air," and I got the message that she wanted to talk privately so I stuffed on dad's old anorak which is what I use for hanging around in, even though it's far too big for me and I nodded to Nat.

I shut the caravan door behind us and jerked my head towards the site entrance. I saw my Uncle Arthur watching us from his trailer – on sites there's always someone on the watch because of intruders. Someone tried to snatch a little girl off one site a bit back – they think just because we're Gyppos it doesn't matter and we're easy targets.

"Come on," I said. "Let's walk towards town and keep our eyes open." As we passed where Dad's old van was parked, I saw a medium spanner on a wall and slipped it into the inside pocket of my anorak. *It would make a good weapon.*

"Yes, it gives us the chance to talk, too," said Nat, "Though I hope you won't need that spanner, because I have an idea. We're going to find the billboard man ."

But as we walked out of the site entrance we met a problem and I realised what the bumblebee sound was.

Twenty Five

To each side of the entrance to the site were those crash barriers police put up, and behind them were TV cameras, press people and lots of onlookers. Entrances to Traveller sites can be quite dangerous as there are often lorries and vans pulling on and off. Today, it felt like we were exhibitions at a freak show and I once even heard a council official say he was 'off to the monkey pen' when he meant he was coming to our site. It does feel like that, people seeing us as different and it felt like it then because there were probably far more gawpers than Press. Several people began shouting – "Any news?" and, "Are you her brother?" Others said, "Poor little mite, living in a place like this. No wonder she went missing."

You see what I mean about Traveller sites? – people think we're less than human and don't have feelings.

"Don't rise to it," Nat muttered and linked her arm through mine, tugging me away. Actually, I hadn't intended to shout back or anything but it just made me feel even sadder. "We'll have to go to my place first, cos there's one or two things I need," she said and I realised she was trying to divert my attention.

"No, I want to go and look for Luckry. I know what she looks like better'n any copper or TV picture."

"Well, I want to search for her, not look for her – it's not the same. Trust me, come on, my place first."

I didn't want to but I've known and trusted Nat for years. Trust is a hard thing to get, especially when you're a Traveller, but Nat had stood by me in all sorts of things so I did what she said and didn't argue. Marshall Meadows caravan site is due west of the town and Nat lives more north west. We crossed the main road which leads into town – London Road – and into the new housing estate where Nat lives. I say new, it's been there about ten years I suppose. They'd given it a posh name, like they always do, to make it sound good – the Hawthorn development – and all the roads were named after trees and shrubs and the houses were one of four type – four and three bedroom detached, two bedroom bungalows and blocks of little flats. Nat lived in one of the three-beds on Willow Rise. Me, I couldn't live in a house like that – it looked like a box and you felt all crowded in by the other houses as if everyone was watching you – give me a site any day. I like to hear the rain on the roof and the owls hooting when I'm in bed and the birds singing in the daytime.

Her house and the others are open plan at the front – I don't like that either – and we just walked up to the front door and Nat let herself in. I stood outside.

"Come in, stupid," she said, but I didn't like to. I heard her shout, "Hello," to her mum and she pushed the door to a bit but so I could still see in, then her mum came to the door.

"Come in, Tom," she said. "Don't wait out there."

I mumbled something but it did no good and I had to, wiping my feet well on the mat and standing on it.

"I'm so sorry to hear about Lucretia," she said. "What a terrible ordeal for you all." I couldn't reply for the lump in my throat which had just come back and the damp spot in the corner of my eye. Nat came downstairs.

"We're going to join the search," she said. "Can you lend me a bit of money? A couple of fivers for preference so we can buy a can and a sarny each.

"Five pounds each? What sort of sandwiches – caviar? Here's one five pound note," and she pulled a note from her purse. Nat gave her a black look.

"You'll get it back," she said,

Her mum gave her a look now. "Come on," and Nat tugging me to the door as I called my goodbyes.

"So what's the plan then?" I asked as we headed back for London Road and the town centre. "I want to find that paedo, that's why I've got the spanner."

"And I want to find him, too, but that spanner won't help. If he really has got Luckry, clobbering him with a spanner will get you into masses of trouble and make sure he either gets off or gets a much shorter sentence. My way, we're either going to do nothing illegal or something only a bit – at least I hope so."

"The plan?"

"We go to World's End Café and we find the billboard paedo. I've got paper, loads of pictures I've printed off of her from the Internet as well as a pen, a torch and a wallet."

I was scornful, I admit it. "The police have been there and searched it and he's not there and neither is Luckry. And how are those things going to help? We got to think where he might have taken her."

"If he's taken her at all. As the cops would say, I want to 'eliminate him from our enquiries' – or not, as the case might be."

Twenty Six

I thought about it and though I still didn't know the plan, I knew Nat had worked out some sort of scheme because that was Nat all over. At school, she was known to be smart – not good at the subjects particularly, though she was all right at most and good at one or two like most of us are, but clever at working things out – a bit like Big Gran in that way I suppose. Main thing is that I've learned to trust her and that when she gives her word, she keeps it. We passed the council offices and ahead of us was Mother Maria's island and the well. If I'd have been on my own, I'd have turned right at the island because that's where the industrial estate is and if you intended to murder – if you wanted to harm a little girl, it'd be a good place to take her. But we turned left and into the town centre. We ignored the shopping mall where kids congregate a lot and kept on the road through the town and to the far end, to the World's End. I think it had been a village once on its own but as the town expanded it got stuck onto the end of it. I've no idea why it was ever called 'World's End'. There was nothing there except a little Co-op, a big charity shop that had anything and everything and the

World's End café which I think depended on people who lived in the flats round there or were doing a bit of grocery shopping or going to the charity shop, which was quite a draw.

"Right," said Nat. "Keep that shut," – and she pointed at my mouth – "Trust me; follow my lead. Right?"

I nodded as she took something from her pocket and fumbled with it.

I followed her inside. It was nothing special as cafés go, an old brown counter with a plastic display case of scones and sandwiches and cakes, a big hot water urn, shelves of cups and saucers and plates and clouds of steam. We approached the counter.

"Yes?" the proprietor asked briefly.

"Excuse me," said Nat, "I wonder if you could help us." He was a man of perhaps sixty with grey hair and glasses who now jerked his chin up for Nat to continue. "You see," she went on, "we were on our way to school when we saw a man with a billboard on his back advertising here and as he walked away we saw he'd dropped something, this wallet thing," and she held out a black credit card holder. "There's no address in but there's a credit card or something and a bit of money, look, she said, half pulling out the fiver her mum had loaned her. "My mum says we've got to give it back to the gentleman." See what I mean about Nat being good at schemes? I'd never have thought of that ruse. "Could we see him please?"

"Oh," said the proprietor, "well he isn't here. Funnily enough," he said, "you're not the first to be looking for him today. We had the – anyway, no he's not here."

Nat gave a big sigh and looked bitterly disappointed. I thought I was getting the plan now. "Oh dear," and she looked like she might cry. "My mum said we had to give it back to him."

"No problem," said the proprietor, "I can give it to him on Saturday. He only works here a bit of the time to advertise it in town and help out on very busy days like Saturday lunch." He held his hand out for the wallet.

Nat pulled it away. "No, my mum said I had to give it to him personally and get a receipt to prove we'd done the right thing as she said we could be accused of theft otherwise and get into lots of trouble."

"I shan't be seeing him before," he replied, "but it'll be perfectly safe here. I promise you."

"But we have to give it to him in his own hands, Mum said. I know, if you would give us his address we'll pop round to where he lives and he might give us a reward." *You crafty girl*, I thought.

"Well," said the proprietor, "I don't know that I should."

"We only want to return his own property and my mum'll kill us if we don't," Nat added for effect, making her eyes look big and a bit scared.

He hesitated. "Well, I suppose there's no harm. Maurice Cleamy – do you know where Battle Way is? It's the blocks of social housing flats."

I didn't, but Nat obviously did: "It's Block 3, fourth floor, room 19." Nat wrote it down.

"Thank you, she said, Thank you very much."

"And here," said the man, "have a bag of crisps each for your honesty."

"Er," I said.

"Thanks," said Nat, giving me a nudge, and took them.

We munched our crisps as we passed back through the main part of town to the big Mother Maria roundabout and went right, heading for the Prospect Industrial estate, the tatty old flats which bordered it and the rescue of Luckry.

Twenty Seven

Nat explained my part in the plan, which was to be the cavalry coming over the hill to the rescue, until finally we got there. "Remember, you'll need to move fast and be very focused ," she said.

Battle Way looked dingy and dark, the sun seemingly ignoring it and casting it under a huge shadow – if the estate where Nat lived looked bad to me, this was more like a prison camp. We passed Block 1 and the twin Block 2 on the way to the triplet Block 3.

"Number 419 ," said Nat as we walked in. "Top floor."

I glanced round, wondering why this block seemed to have escaped any damage at all from the quake, as far as I could tell. Nat pressed the button for the lift and we waited, reading the graffiti which idiots had added, stuff about girls and boys, racist things, all sorts of nonsense but often a name (like Jack) a heart and another name (like Kate). A few had a rude word in the middle of the heart. We Travellers – well, Romanies – don't like that sort of thing in mixed company so in front of Nat I found it embarrassing, but Nat didn't seem to care. There were quite a few bits of rubbish lying around, old polystyrene trays and beakers from takeaways, crisp packets, and cans. Do you know, you could go on our site any hour of the day and not pick up more than five bits of rubbish on the whole site and they say we're dirty.

When the lift failed to arrive after five minutes, we realized it wasn't working and set off up the drab concrete stairs, set out in alternate blocks of twelve and six, which seemed to smell of rank urine and old smoke and I don't care to think what else.

"I'm psyching myself up – I don't want to blow it," I said as we reached the fourth floor.

"And keep that spanner in your pocket; no stupidity right?" Nat ordered.

I knew she was right, but it was comforting to think that it was there, nestling in the big anorak if I needed a weapon. I hoped she was right that it wouldn't be necessary.

At the top of the stairs, a grubby and battered board pointed the directions for rooms – 1-10 to the right and 11-20 on the left. We went through the shabby fire door, which at least still seemed to be working and closing as a fire door should, and checked off the numbers. We didn't need to go far along the corridor as No. 19 was immediately opposite No. 12 and so only the second flat along, which meant that we wouldn't have to run far to get back to the stairs with Luckry. I'd got it into my mind that if she was there she might have been drugged or injured and that I'd have to carry her down four flights of stairs at a run with the man chasing us.

Nat was about to ring the bell.

"Wait," I said. I pushed my ear to the door and listened intently, but I could hear nothing. I thought I might hear a crying child or even the telly. Nat handed me her scarf and I wrapped it round my face so only my eyes showed and half knotted the ends behind my neck. Then I flattened against the wall so I couldn't be seen from the doorway. Nat rang.

We heard someone coming to the door and as soon as he answered, Nat said, "Excuse me, sir, sorry to trouble you, but are you Mr. Cleamy, Mr. Maurice Cleamy?" She half proffered the wallet.

"Yes." The man sounded uncertain, as well he might be, but he had worse to come. I sprang, leaping from my place behind the wall, pushed past him with my left hand, ran down a tiny corridor passing two doors on my left and one on the right and so towards an open door ahead.

"Oy! What the ..." he shouted.

"Luckry, Luckry," I called. "It's Blotch. Where are you?" I forged ahead and found myself in a little sitting room.

"Luckry!"

It took no search to see she was not there and nor in the adjoining mini kitchen. I backtracked towards the other rooms as Mr. Cleamy came into his sitting room. I pushed him hard and he staggered back, banging himself against the doorframe and stumbling and falling. Then I was past him and pushing open the bathroom door, where again there was no sign, threw open a utility room door holding only a vac' and so into the opposite bedroom.

"Luckry!"

Twenty Eight

There was little in the room. A single bed, the covers pulled immaculately over, a chair by the bed, a little bedside table and a wardrobe. I could see no Luckry was in the bed and a quick peer under it proved she wasn't there either. I dived for the wardrobe and almost threw the door off its hinges in my haste. "Luckry, Luckry!" All it contained were a couple of shirts and two pairs of trousers. The cupboard was bare – no Luckry, nothing else.

In my distress I was finding it hard to breathe so I pulled Nat's scarf from my face, slumped onto the bed and cried my very heart out. The grief, the worry, the awful guilt, the helplessness all seemed to hit me at once. I sobbed and sobbed, pouring tears and retching. I no longer cared about Mr. Cleamy or what he might tell the police about me forcing my way in: if he had taken Luckry, she was not there and no matter what I did, he wasn't going to tell me where he had dumped her. Nat sat by me, tucked her arm round me, shushed me, and pulled me tightly to her so I could hear her heart in between my sobs.

"Shhhh, it's OK, we'll find her ," she soothed.

Mr. Cleamy sat at the far side of me. "I think I understand – it's your sister gone missing, isn't it." A statement not a question. "You thought it was me, that she was here." I didn't reply. "Just because I shouted about looking after her, it doesn't make me a kidnapper you know."

"It wasn't just that: you're a paedo and you said one day we might lose her ," Nat said, firmly. "That's why we came. How did you know she was going to go missing?"

"I didn't know – I just thought you weren't looking after her very well when that boy tugged her and she stumbled. No, I made a wicked mistake. I'm not a peadophile just a man who, who was stupid and did the wrong thing some years ago, but I never actually harmed any children, I swear. I wouldn't, couldn't. I've not seen your sister at all since I saw her with you, I swear again."

Maybe a bit of Big Gran Lucretia had got into me, but somehow I knew he was telling the truth and the awfulness of what we'd just done – I'd done – hit me. "If I could help, I would," he went on, "and by the way, the police have already been here and searched. They didn't have a warrant, but because I was innocent I wanted them to so I could clear myself of suspicion."

"I'm sorry ," I whispered, "I was sure it was you who'd taken her and with you saying something about her getting lost – but I'm sorry. I'd no right to burst in here and scare you like I did. I don't know what to do now, any more."

What I had done began to hit me and I glared at Nat.

"I'll put the radio on ," said Mr. Cleamy. "Local news, see if there's any new information." He went through into the living room and we heard the radio. After a few moments, he returned with a glass of water and pushed it into my hand. My sobs were diminishing.

"No, nothing, sorry. But look, young man and young lady, what you did was very, very wrong. You had no right at all and you made guesses and assumptions which were wicked and ridiculous. If I went to the police you'd get done for assault and burglary or something, do you know that?" I nodded. "When I fell, I could have been injured – I wasn't thankfully. And if you'd brought a weapon ..." The words hovered over me like an executioner's sword because I somehow suspected that he had guessed that I would have done and the spanner suddenly felt very heavy in the coat. I opened my mouth to confess that it was exactly what I had done when Nat came to the rescue.

"We're very sorry, both of us. Please don't go to the police. We misjudged you, we know that now but I'm sure you can understand the enormous stress and fear that Tom is under. We can only ask you, plead with you, to forgive us both. We want to go and continue our search and not have to stop and explain ourselves to the police. We know we were wrong. Sorry." Nat picked up her scarf. Can we go now?"

What would have happened had he said 'no', I daren't think. Because I'm sure Nat would have exploded, wrong or not, and we certainly wouldn't have stayed. He nodded, and we made for the bedroom and then the flat doors.

"Goodbye ," said Nat. "Thank you. Sorry again."

"Sorry," I added.

"What now?" I asked as Nat shut the door. "That was a disaster."

"Yes, it was unfortunate but we can probably assume he's not involved. So now, we keep searching. As I say, I don't think he did take her, but it's still possible someone else did. First, we make some rough posters using the pictures and put them up at the entrances to these flats because they seem very unsavoury to me, then we make a new plan."

Twenty Nine

We put two pictures up at the entrance to each of the blocks of flats and Nat wrote on each, 'Please help us to find this missing little girl, Lucretia Morrison. If you think you've seen her or can help, contact the police.'

We set off back towards the Mother Maria roundabout, but Nat wanted us to go into town to the shopping mall itself. She had this theory that two kids asking the public because they were trying to find a child would attract more sympathy than the police and might make people think more deeply if they'd seen her.

We stuck together and stationed ourselves outside one of the big clothes stores so we could catch lots of people and we each approached passers-by.

"Excuse me; have you seen this missing child today please?"

Most women and old aged people stopped and at least had a look at the picture.

"No ducks, sorry – good luck."

"Oh saw that on the telly, no, sorry."

"She your sister then?"

One or two said, "Too busy," or "Train to catch," and rushed on, mainly younger men.

At last, I found one I thought could help and just as I was talking to her, the mutt dog came up to me and pushed its snout into the back of my leg. I didn't let it distract me.

The woman was getting on, perhaps in her 60s. She put down her shopping bag and stared at the photo, pulling it first close to her eyes and then to arm's length.

"Hmmm ," she said, "It's no good; I shall have to put my specs on."

She fiddled about in her coat pocket, produced a pair and swopped them over whilst my anticipation, hope and frustration all rose. "Now let's see." She nodded, "Yes, in school uniform wasn't she?"

"Well, PE things actually, black shorts and a white singlet."

"Yes, that's right, school uniform, blue gingham, she was just sitting over there," and she indicated a low wall round a statue of someone. "Yesterday I saw her, with some more from that school."

"No, no ," I said. "Today – we're trying to find her today because she's gone missing *today* ," and I almost shouted the crucial word.

"Yes, that's right ," she concluded, "a little boy, yesterday, with his mum and some more."

"Thank you," I said, and approached someone else.

Nat seemed to be having no more luck than I. Most people just shook their heads, a few studied the picture but it was obvious that no one had seen her.

"It's hopeless ," I said to Nat. !We're wasting our time and if she's been snatched we're losing precious time."

Nat held my arm. "Look, I've a feeling she hasn't been taken by someone, but in any case the police will have got that side well and truly covered, as we found when we went to that Mr. Cleamy's. We're better here in the hope of finding a clue as to which way she went and the shopping mall's a good place to catch people and the sort of place Luckry would go if she had fifteen quid in her pocket to spend for some reason. I'm going to go and ask the staff in that café that does special food for kids. Hang on, why's that dog back again? You got a piece of meat in your pocket or something; it keeps muzzling you all the time."

While she was going to the café, I decided to try some of the shops selling things Luckry might have wanted the money for, not the places that sold sneakers because the police had done them, but the ones that sold little girly things like pictures of weird pop stars and cartoon characters, toys and stickers and pencils and stuff. I'd just done my third when I saw Nat coming back and with her was another old lady tugging a fabric shopping trolley.

"Tom ," she called, and beckoned me over. "This lady thinks she's seen her earlier on."

"Well ," said the woman, "I can't be sure. It may have been a boy I saw. She was wearing black shorts and a white top with the school badge and I noticed that she had

114

one shoe on and one PE pump which I thought was strange, but I didn't really see her face ..." I think at that point my heart stopped. "It was the dog, too, that scruffy one over there. It was walking with her, cos, I thought to myself, a little child like that shouldn't be out on her own, all sorts of things could happen."

"Where was she?" I asked, yearning for a fast reply.

"Just over there ," she said, "far side of the roundabout. I spoke to her cos I was worried but she said she was all right."

"Thank you, thank you very much ," I said, and started to run towards the roundabout. Fortunately Nat didn't join me because she was still listening to the old woman.

"Wait a minute ," the woman shouted; "Don't you want to know where she said she was going?"

Thirty

I stopped in my tracks and came back. "Sorry ," I said. "I'm just so worried."

"She was over the far side of the roundabout as if she'd come from the school ," the shopper continued. I wanted to tell her to hurry up, that it was urgent, that time wasn't on our side. "She had that dog with her. I thought maybe she was lost. I said to her, 'You all right ducks?' and she said she was and I said, 'Where you off to? Do you parents know where you are?' and she said she was going to the wishing well cos she had to do something for her brother. Well, I watched her then and she crossed on the walking man crossing and the dog was next to her leg the whole time and I thought that's well trained, it almost looked glued to her. I saw her get to the island. Oh and I found this, I don't know if it was hers."

She passed me the clincher – a silver hair slide in the shape of a flat horse. "I found it on the pavement."

"Thank you," I said. "Thank you very much. We must find her."

"When did you see her?" ever practical Nat asked. "About how long ago?"

"Oh, let's see," said the woman. "I reckon it was several hours ago, cos it was this morning."

"Thank you, thank you very much," I said again. "Please excuse us, we're very worried about her and must find her."

I ran off towards the island with Nat hard on my heels. "Hang on!" she shouted after me, but I took no notice.

Although it's now a very large traffic island, Mother Maria's Well has several pedestrian crossings to it exactly because it is such a landmark in the town and lots go there – especially kids – to make a wish and two of the ways across even have those green cross crossings where you press a button. There's also a zebra crossing. I can't say Luckry's brilliant in traffic, being only six, but she's not bad and it fitted that she would have crossed at the proper place. *In any case,* I reasoned, *if she'd met with an accident on the road later on, the police'd have known already.* So for Luckry to get to it would have been easy, though once there she could have got back just as easily which meant we may be on yet another wild goose chase.

I couldn't wait for the light to go green and ran across, dodging traffic and angry motorists. Nat did it the proper way, but by the time she reached me I was already at the well and frantically looking for Luckry.

The well's almost in the middle of the island and there are paths which go round and across the island, radiating out from the well. I ran down several, looking and calling, but there was no sign. Near the well are a couple of benches where people tend to sit who have taken kids there but no one was on them now. There's an underground stream which feeds the well and runs from it in the opposite direction – I don't know where the water goes in the end, the river I expect. A quick dash and a second search of the island showed that it, was, indeed, another fruitless venture.

I stared at the well. I wonder if she could be down there?

Nat shook her head and tugged at the steel grill over the top of the well. "Have you forgotten? The police checked it. She can't possibly be down there. It's solid and well padlocked and no one could have pulled it off, least of all a six year old who would have also had to have had the means to put it back and re-padlock it."

My heart sank to my boots. Nat was right – so Luckry couldn't possibly be down the well. "So where is she? I keep getting this terrifying thought that she must have been snatched. If I could get my hands on them ..." I left the thought unanswered. "What the ...?"

Something warm and furry rubbed against my leg.

"I don't believe it! It's that stupid dog! How did it get here? I'll swear it's following me," I said agitatedly. "Go, on, shoo," and I made as if to chase it.

"Look! It's holding a school PE ball in its mouth. If it thinks I'm playing with it now, it must be daft. Get lost!" Nat shouted.

The dog thumped its tail against my leg again. I felt sorry for it and automatically stroked the dog's head.

"I think it's just glad to be with people," I said. "It was with Luckry earlier – if only it could talk. It probably thinks we're just on a walk and have some biscuits or something. It looks half starved, like a stray. Where's it off now?"

It trotted away towards one end of the traffic island and slumped down, as if exhausted. "Flash your torch down the well, will you Nat – just in case there's a clue?" but I'd actually given up hope. When she did, just for a fleeting moment I thought I saw something white.

"What the ...?" Not when there'd been no sign before; not when hope had already fled; not when she couldn't possibly have got in there. *Ridiculous*, I thought, *it can't be anything to do with her*.

"Shine again." It wasn't actually dark down the well, just gloomy.

"Luckry?" I said the name softly, as if I couldn't really believe I'd seen anything. Nat flashed the torch down the well but its beam was not quite powerful enough though I could see something, a piece of paper? A piece of cloth?

"Luckry?" More loudly now. "Luckry? Is that you?" I knew it wasn't, but I was just desperate.

And then the unbelievable, the answering voice!

"Blotch? 'S'that you? I don't like it here! I'm cold, very cold. I fell asleep and now I want to go to sleep again. But it's cold."

Thirty One

The realisation struck me harder than a boxer's fist – Luckry was alive after all and very close!

"Luckry! Luckry!" I screamed. "Luckry! I'm coming Luckry! Listen! I'm coming for you! Where are you?"

"I'm here!"

Her voice sounded hollow and echoed. It shook with uncertainty, as if she wasn't sure if I was really there. In my own panic and fear, I almost screamed with frustration.

"It's Blotch. Listen, I'm coming for you. I need to know ..." I tried to work out the words exactly so as not to panic her ... "Luckry! Are you all right?"

"Hurry up!" said Luckry. "I can't get out." It sounded closer. Had I really found her or was it some trick of my mind?

Ever practical, Nat pointed at the padlock and called, "Luckry, I'm here too. We want to get you out – tell us how you got in there so we can come? Did someone put you there?"

"Yes," she moaned, almost uncertainly.

"How did he get you in there? Did he have a key for the padlock?" I shouted.

"Who?"

"Whoever put you in there?"

"Who did?"

"For crying out loud," said Nat. "You can have this conversation later. Just reassure her and tell her help is on the way. Take my torch."

"They must have had a key to the padlock, otherwise the police would have seen it missing," I said. "It's a wonder she wasn't killed, throwing her in there. If I ever get them I'll kill them with my own two hands." I turned but Nat was no longer there – I thought she'd gone for help.

I tried to reassure Luckry, "I'll soon be there, sis," I called excitedly, "and Nat's gone for the fire brigade. Soon be with you!" I said.

The mutt of a dog rubbed against me again and licked my hand. "You," I said to the dog, "are going to be the sorriest dog on this planet in a moment. I've got better things to do." I kicked out at it but it was too fast for me.

"Luckry," I called again. "Don't go to sleep. When we get you home and warm you can sleep then as long as you want." I'd read somewhere that trapped people shouldn't be allowed to fall asleep but I didn't know why. "Luckry?"

I flashed Nat's torch to get a better view. I could just about see Luckry huddled on what looked like a gravel mound at the side of the water but the pile wasn't big enough to take all of her, even though she was squashed up, and I thought her feet looked slightly dipped into the pool. I could see coins lying about in the water, and occasionally on ledges on the walls, too.

"Luckry?" I asked. "How did you get in there?"

"Over here, over here."

I rushed over to where Nat was calling from. The dog was there, lying next to Nat on part of the traffic island which was higher than the rest. "The dog showed me where it was," Nat explained. "Look."

She pointed to a large old metal drain cover, so ancient it was hardly noticeable with a broken fossilised padlock attached to it, obviously to keep it unsuccessfully locked. The hatchway was half hidden from the outside by a Grade A listed patch of nettles which I'd just found the hard way. How Luckry had got through them and lifted the cover I couldn't imagine, unless, of course, someone had done it for her and forced her in, which was still my fear.

I peered down the hatchway about two feet down underground and I could see the stream which obviously led to the well.

I rushed back to the top of the well to tell Luckry what we'd found and to reassure her. Before I could speak, there was a splashing somewhere below and when I shone the torch down to the bottom of the well, expecting to vaguely see Luckry moving about, I got a shock. Luckry was still huddled at the side of the well but beside her was the mutt, licking Luckry as fast as it could.

"Stop it," I heard Luckry say. "Stop it, leave me alone. I don't like my face licked."

If I'd had a brick handy I'd have lobbed it at the dog. It's one of our Romany things that dogs aren't allowed to lick people or anything used by people, especially not on the face. Mind, I was so steamed up it was a good job I hadn't got something to throw because through the mesh I'd probably have missed the dog and hit Luckry. I feared the dog was on the brink of biting her. Then it dawned on me – it was keeping Luckry awake and not letting her sleep and probably warming her face in the process: which left one odd question and an enormous one – why was it doing it? It must have gone along the tunnel to reach her and that meant that if it could and Luckry could, maybe I could too.

Thirty Two

"Stop it, go away," but the dog ignored her and kept licking for all it was worth.

Nat shouted, "I'm going for help."

"The dog's got to her," I shouted back. "It's licking her face all the time. I don't like it but maybe it's helping her." I flashed the torch so I could see the animal still licking for all it was worth. Not very hygienic but it must have realised what she needed.

"More to the point, *how* did the dog get to her?" asked Nat. "And can we use the same route? It must be along a pipe but Luckry and the dog are smaller than we are." Then she was gone for the help.

I trotted over to the far side of the island where I didn't think any further – I sat on the edge of the hatchway and stood on the bottom. The water swirled round my ankles but no further up. At least it wasn't deep. I dropped myself into it and then discovered it wasn't a tunnel at all but simply a wide pipe, angled down. Luckry might just have got on it in a crouching frog position but it was too small for me: the only way was to lie down in the water with my head towards the well and try to move along, pushing myself with my feet and half dragging by wedging my hands against the side and heaving and half sort of swimming. The moment I lay down, I felt the icy water pushing me from behind and it was quite easy to move through, with an air space above, except for the extreme cold. I'd estimated about fifteen metres from the drain cover to the bottom of the well and I'd done about five when I found a problem. The pipe took a sudden steep angle down – a little waterfall. By now, there was almost no light so I couldn't actually estimate how far down it went but as the water was running towards the well I guessed it couldn't be more than a metre at most and probably less, but I wasn't going to stop now. Cautiously, my arms and hands stretched in front of me, I angled down the pipe but the water was now rushing over my head and breathing had become far more difficult. I slid down the pipe to the bottom and banged my head on something – enough to hurt, but thankfully no more. Then I was on the slightly reclining stretch again. The adrenalin or something was pumping and I got increasingly frightened at not getting air easily, and what would happen if I reached somewhere that the air ran out so I pulled and pushed myself frantically forward as fast as I could.

Suddenly, ahead of me I saw dim light and guessed it was the bottom of the well ahead of me.

"I'm coming, Luckry, I'm coming," I spluttered. I gave a final push and a pull and splooshed and splurted my way into open space. Huddled on a pile of gravel at the side of the well was Luckry, the dog still licking for all it was worth.

"I'm here Luckry," I called and started a coughing fit because of the water I'd swallowed and which was still dribbling over my face.

"I want to go home!" an obviously frightened and fed up Luckry wailed.

"It's OK, Luckry, OK. I'm here with you. We'll be fine," I whispered, grasping her arms. I was going to clutch her to me but realised my clothes were soaking with water whereas she seemed more damp than wet because, I reasoned, she'd dried out a bit from her wetting and had probably managed to crawl through the pipe rather than lie down.

"Don't worry my love, Nat's gone for help. It'll be here soon. You see, I don't think I can get you out the way you came. The water will rush into our faces."

"I know," she said. "I tried. And there's a big metal thing over the other side so I couldn't go that way." It was another metal grill, obviously intended to stop waste or debris going any further and indeed stuff was piled against it like an inefficient dam.

"I think we'll just have to wait for the rescuers now," I said. "They won't be very long. Nat, are you back?" I called up the shaft.

A beam of light flashed down. "Emergency people are on the way. What's the situation? Is she hurt?" Nat called.

It hadn't crossed my mind to check, but at a quick glance she looked fine except she was shaking and shuddering violently. I pulled her tightly now against my anorak and realised my mistake so I undid my anorak, pulled her again into it and against my chest, and zipped it up with her pressed against me.

Luckry's wailing changed down a gear to sobbing. "I want to go home! I'm cold."

"I know, I said. Luckry, did a bad man make you go in here?"

"No, Big Gran said I had to."

It was a conversation going nowhere and the main thing was she was alive and would soon be safe. She felt damp, though not actually wet, but my trousers were sodden and water seemed to have somehow cascaded down the back of my anorak and my back. But at least the front of me was a bit warm and dry inside the anorak.

Thirty Three

"Hey!" Nat shouted down. "If her clothes are wet, take them off."

I felt a flash of anger. "Stupid that'll make her even colder. And you're supposed to keep clothes on even if they say they're hot."

"Catch," Nat called. In the beam of the torch a scarf fluttered down.

"Idiot!" I shouted. "What good's a scarf? She needs blankets." I caught it.

"Listen, double idiot. You're forgetting the big metal grill which is over the top of this well. The holes are far too small to get anything through unless you can screw it up. It's my sister's college scarf – it's long and wide and wool so just flatten it out and wrap it round her like an Egyptian mummy."

"Sorry," I whispered, choking back tears of fear, guilt and frustration. I unzipped my anorak and tried to stuff the scarf round Luckry but it didn't seem to work well and certainly wouldn't flatten out as Nat had suggested, but I thought it might just help a bit. I kept holding her in my anorak as tightly as I could.

I was beginning to feel very cold myself. I couldn't imagine how Luckry had managed so long down here. I started shivering, or maybe her shiver was infectious. I couldn't do anything about her feet because I was already crouched in the water myself. My feet were astonishingly cold, so heaven knows what hers were like. I just wanted to keep her as warm as I could.

I don't know if Luckry heard the sirens or not, but Nat did and called down.

"They're nearly here."

I was too cold and tired to answer. Also, whilst I realised the dog was trying to help with its attempts at licking and nuzzling, it was becoming a bit of a nuisance. Luckry had fallen asleep and I knew that as a bad thing but I just couldn't wake her. I dunno, maybe the dog was making a fuss to stop her sleeping, somehow sensing she mustn't yet. It couldn't get to her face any more as hers was pressed against me but paddled in the water and tongued the back of her legs for all it was worth.

There was a sound of a bolt-cutter scrunch at the top and I heard the metal grill fly off. Strong lights shone down on us both. A figure in a white helmet peered down.

"Help!" I shouted. "Help! Down here!" as if it wasn't obvious.

"We're on our way, only a few moments now," he said.

"The dog's real pleased to see me. It wants to give me a bath! Stop it, doggie!" It was Luckry talking and coherently – well, reasonably so. At least she was conscious and awake. "I've hurt my lip," she said. I couldn't possibly see because she was pressed to me and it was too dark anyway. She sobbed a little, I suspected more for sympathy than anything else but perhaps I was being hard.

"It's all right sweetie. Tell me how you hurt the lip?" I asked, more to occupy her and keep her awake.

"I banged it in that tunnel. I fell down a slope. It was steep." I guessed where she meant at the angle where the pipe suddenly went down.

"It's OK," I reassured her. "We'll soon be out."

"I got the coin back," she said. I'd forgotten all about it. "Big Gran's gold coin. I wished for something very big and it happened, but Big Gran didn't want me to leave the coin here so I came to get it back."

She couldn't have wished for an earthquake – could she? No! "Won't be long now," I reassured her.

"Hurry up, Blotch, I want to go home. Big Gran says you should have been here a long time ago – she told you what was going to happen," Luckry added.

The man in the white helmet called: "We're putting a ladder down into the water, next to you. Stay there, don't try to come up because we're coming to you. Is she hurt?"

"I don't think so," I said. "Except her lip."

"We can't take the chance. Are you OK?"

"Yes, fine, except being cold."

A ladder slowly lowered down and stood in the water behind me. There isn't much room, I called. A fireman slid down – it took him about two seconds and I wished I could go safely down a ladder that fast. A second man followed but stopped before the bottom. He had a little stretcher thing.

"Hello," he said to Luckry. "Let's get you back up." He took her gently from my now unzipped coat and he and the other man put her on the little stretcher and strapped her in. The whole thing took no more than a few seconds. I watched as they pulled her up. Then it was my turn. "Can't take any chances," and another stretcher came down. There wasn't room to lie it down but they angled it and slid me onto it and once more straps and a head brace were tightened.

"I'm all right," I protested but they took no notice and a moment later I was out of the top and laid, still, on the stretcher, on the ground. The dog followed in a fireman's arms.

Thirty four

Out of the corner of my eye I could see Luckry wrapped in a silver blanket and looking like an alien doll. Mum was with her and as I watched they loaded Luckry with Mum almost glued to her heels into an ambulance and away they went.

"I'm OK," I said. "Just banged my leg in the school, but it's only a bruise and my head a bit in that pipe, but it's just that I'm cold. Really, no need to ..."

"Good," said a paramedic, missing what I wanted him to do – to just let me go home. Then it was my turn to get the turkey wrap treatment and as they did it I saw, out of the corner of my eye, that there was a third stretcher on the ground. Whoever was on that wasn't in the special blanket, but I could plainly see a neck brace and I'd know that face anywhere and especially the curved French plaits fastened at each side of her head.

"Nat," I called. "What's happened?"

She didn't answer, but I could hear her chuntering in typical Nat style. "… Perfectly all right, just banged my head a bit, get me off this thing …"

Then Dad was beside me. "Are you all right, son? You're a hero! You saved her life, probably."

Dad and I went in a second ambulance with a prostrate and cross Nat for company.

They didn't put the siren on, but I could see the reflection of the blue light. "What happened?" I asked Nat.

"Nothing much," she growled. "When you went into Luckry's school and the doorframe came down, the door frame clouted me on the head."

"You never said."

"My head wasn't important, it was Luckry we were there for and then when we were in the hall searching and a lump of plaster came down, it ricocheted off the floor and clobbered me again. I'm perfectly all right, but will they listen?"

She didn't look all right. My neck brace stopped me from turning my head, but when I twisted my eyes, she was on a bed at the opposite side of the ambulance with a metal frame up to stop her falling off and I realised so was I. Her face was very pale and there was a distinct smear of blood down the left of her cheek.

"I just felt a bit dizzy that's all," she continued. "I fell over and everyone panicked."

"Nat?" I asked.

"What?"

"You're a hero. Thanks for helping get my sister back."

"Hmmm," she answered. "Be kinder to her next time. Now shut up."

I thought I could see a little damp patch in the corner of her eye and realised I had one too. Then Dad was asking me exactly what had happened but I was more concerned about finding out about Luckry.

"She's fine, thanks to you two," he said. "Touch of hypothermia but nothing to worry about. You got to her in time – oh and a thick lip."

Naturally, at the hospital, Luckry had the first check over and Dad told me that Luckry (with Mum) had been admitted to a ward for treatment for Luckry's mild hypothermia and 'observation.' Then it was Nat's turn and I expect the waiting time in A and E got even longer as we three had all the preferential treatment. Later Dad told me they'd given her a good check-up and the head injury was only mild concussion, thank goodness.

My turn came next and they did an X-ray of my neck as a precaution but there was no problem. They saw the big bruise on my leg from the falling doorframe, which was nothing, and the cuts and scuffs on my hands from the digging, but really I was the best of the three, just still very cold. They bundled me off to a general ward and told me I had to stay in overnight 'for observation' though I couldn't see the need any more than Nat could.

They stripped my clothes off me and then sent me for a lovely hot bath. Meanwhile, Dad nipped to the site and brought me some different warm clothes and night things (and an illicit sausage cob) so after the bath I snuggled into a lovely big hospital bed, dressings all over my hands from the damage caused by the digging, and had a huge bowl of soup and a hot chocolate drink to settle the cob. The thing is, undressing or being partly dressed are more of those things we Romanies think important and sort of 'not nice', so even though I was behind the curtain screen I was embarrassed due to lady nurses helping and other patients not related being in the ward, too.

Dad wasn't allowed to stay with me overnight, not that I'd have wanted him to, but apparently Mum popped her head in later on when Luckry had fallen asleep, but by then, I was fast asleep myself.

Thirty Five

When I awoke, the sun was shining and everywhere birds seemed to be singing. I remembered where I was, hutched myself up onto one elbow and stared round the ward. I was the youngest there by a lifetime. An old wrinkled man opposite with a face like flour was fast asleep. In the bed near me was another old man sitting up and apparently mummified with bandages. I was sorry for them both but I couldn't help feeling like a million quid myself. I felt free after all we'd gone through, like waking into heaven and having got a massive reward of my sister back and safe. My only question was how Luckry and Nat were today after their ordeal.

I wanted the curtains dawn round me so no-one could look at me but a nurse said they had to be able to see if I was OK every time they popped into the ward and that was also why they'd been open all night (which I'd also found unpleasant).

For breakfast I had my favourite cereals and *three* slices of toast – apparently the ration's supposed to be two, but old Mr. Somebody had only wanted one so I got his!

After breakfast, Mum came to see me and I got the biggest hug I've ever had in my life. The nurses said she could take me to see Luckry who was sitting up in bed in a children's ward looking at a book. I got another big hug there and she looked fine to me. They told me to go back to my ward as the doctor was on the way.

Before the doctor arrived, half the site walked in to see me bearing bunches of flowers, chocolate, grapes (yuck!), cans and sweets and, with Dad, another unofficial sausage cob. That's what we Romanies do when someone's ill because everyone wants to go and see them and check they're OK and get them anything they need (whether they actually need it or not). Granny Rayni's contribution was the largest box of chocolates I'd ever seen in my life, not that I complained. But it wasn't visiting time and the nurses shooed everyone out – I think someone getting 18 visitors was a bit much for them.

I was still waiting for the doctor when I had another visitor – Nat! "Get up, lazy!" she said. She was in a hospital nightgown which looked far too long and a funny looking candlewick dressing gown which I think must have been her mum's. Her head was bandaged. I explained that I'd wanted to get up, of course, but other than the little visit they'd let me make to Luckry, they said I had to stay in bed until after the doctor.

"The doc's seen me already," Nat announced. "They gave me a good check-up and decided I was human after all, despite having you as a reckless friend. Actually, they said I could go home after lunch – mild concussion and a cut only."

"So why the bandage and not a plaster?" I showed her the assortment I had on my own hands from the digging.

"Because they'd have had to cut a lump out of my hair for one of these stupid modern head dressings, so I said I'm not losing part of a pigtail for anyone and they compromised."

"But why didn't I see the blood when your head got hit?" I asked.

"Because," she said, "I'd got so much plaster dust in my hair it hid it until the blood seeped through."

"You're a hero, Nat," I said.

"Shut up," she replied. "Anyone bring you any chocolate? My mum didn't. Total let down. I mean, if you've got to be in hospital it's the thing you have to have to get better."

I tried to get away with passing her the grapes.

"Don't be ridiculous," she said. "I know enough about Travellers to work out you've got more chocolate than the chocolate factory somewhere. Get it out!" she said, bending down and pulling the massive chocolate box from where I thought I'd hidden it under the bed. "At least your little sister's got the generous streak which missed you," and I knew then that Luckry had also had a mass visitation of family.

Nat sat on my bed and we munched and swigged cans until a nurse came and said we were making too much noise and disturbing the other patients. All I can say is they didn't *look* upset, we were entertaining them and they were enjoying the spectacle and our banter.

When the doctor finally came, Nat had to do a quick retreat back to her ward, taking some of the booty with her. He quickly decided I was doing fine and could get dressed and go home after dinner and as soon as I had got my clothes on, I went off to see Luckry and Nat in their ward.

Nat's mum was there and she asked how I was and said how brave I had been to rescue my sister.

"It was Nat," I said. "Without her, I couldn't have done any of it."

"Shut up," said Nat. "Or do you want a slap?"

Thirty Six

It never crossed my mind that I might be a celebrity. All I'd done was what anyone would do – help save their baby sister. A nurse took all three of us – Luckry, Nat and me – to the main entrance and with us was Nat's mum and my mum and Dad and Karen. As we walked out into the fresh air and freedom (OK, I know the hospital helped us but to me it was like being in a sort of open prison) I stopped in my tracks.

"What the ...?" I began.

A crowd of people stood behind a cordon which seemed to be mainly kids from our school and an occasional teacher and they were cheering and whistling and clapping and then the cordon seemed to part in the middle and the scruffy dog came hurtling towards us. Whining and yelping all the way, it made a bee-line for Luckry and I feared it would leap at her, but it didn't. It thrust its head to her and began trying to lick, but it could only easily get to her hands as she had a pair of trousers and a coat on this time.

"I'm all OK, silly dog," she said. "Have you missed me?"

I felt tears in my eyes, but they were tears of relief and joy which kept trying to bubble into the open. And the press were there and TV, especially filming Luckry and the dog and they were coming up wanting to ask me questions and also Luckry and Nat.

Karen said, "I have an agreed statement here from the children's parents which I am going to read. We want to get the children to their homes to fully recuperate but it may be possible to grant controlled interviews in a few days." Then she read the statement you have already about how brave Nat and I had been and how everybody was proud of us and how lovely that the little 'princess' was safe but that we just wanted to get back to our normal lives now. All the time, the film cameras were on us.

A medic lifted Luckry into the back of Uncle Arthur's four-by-four (they must have thought stuffing her in Dad's van wasn't the best of images). They trundled Nat – head still bandaged – into her mum's car, still saying was fine but no one taking any notice, Nat chuntering the whole time.

"Will someone just listen!" she grumbled. "There's nothing wrong with my head. It's just a bit sore, that's all!"

I chuckled, and felt damp in the corners of my eyes again.

I got in the back beside Luckry, then we were off, Nat back to her place and me and Luckry back to the site.

There were even people here and there who waved. Karen was in a police car behind us.

"It's been on the local news," Mum said. "So people knew you'd all be coming out of hospital. I just thank God you're all OK – you and Natalie rushing in to save your kid sister. They came to see a hero!"

"What?" I really didn't understand. "Not me. Anybody would have!"

You really couldn't see there'd been a mini earthquake, there was just no sign. I suppose the odd loose tile might have come off a roof but there was nothing at all obvious until I thought about Luckry's school and why that had come off so badly – still, not so badly, because no one had been hurt and Luckry wouldn't have got into difficulties if she hadn't put herself there.

"Luckry's school got it worst," I observed, "But why? There must have been a fault right under where the schools are or somewhere close by."

The car stopped very suddenly. "Damn dog!" my uncle said, but I knew exactly which dog it was even without looking. What's more, on the pavement was a man who was all too familiar – one with a billboard.

"Heh!" I said. "That's the man I thought had taken her – still there! 'The end of the world is nigh!' A bit late, mate, it's been and gone – and your message should read, 'Tough, you missed your cup of tea at the World's End' – I could murder a cup of mengri" – our word for tea – "myself right now!"

The animal sat forlornly right in front of the car stopping us going and ignoring the horn until, finally, it shuffled to the side of the road until we got past, then when I looked behind it was haring after us at full pelt and I could see something in its mouth and hanging out of it.

"What's it got?" I wondered aloud.

Luckry had realised, too, who the dog was. "Good doggie!" Luckry shouted at the top of her voice.

The dog must have heard her call. Its tail beat wildly a couple of times and it loped after the car.

"That dog might be the scruffiest and daftest animal in Britain," I said, "but it's still a hero."

"I don't think it's just the dog!" said Mum, turning round from the front and squeezing and hugging me weakly from a distance. "Are you sure you're OK?"

"Nearly back to normal!" I said and sighed, wishing Nat was there to give one of her cutting comments.

Thirty Seven

"They reckon it was the chemicals they'd pumped into Marshall Meadows," Dad said. "The pressure built up in natural faults. That caused the 'quake. I don't think they realised what could happen. That's what their theory is saying, anyway, but they're going to have to do some work to find the cause because it could be the fracking too."

"That just about tallies with my luck for the day!" I sighed. "I knew something bad was happening with the barking dogs and the hens and the bubbling water and so on. I just knew it was going to get worse so I should've known it'd end up like this!"

"You were horrid to me yesterday until you came back for me!" Luckry reminded me.

"Yeah, I know and I'm sorry. But I tried to make up for it, I really did! I tried to be responsible for her, Mum, like you always say."

"Responsible!" Mum's eyes went wide. "You deserve a medal!"

"No, everyone chipped in. Nat, the rescuers – and the dog! Have we lost it or is it still behind?"

"I can't see it any more," Uncle said. "I think it's got too tired and the police stopped to get it. Pity, I think we owe it one for what it did and if it is a stray maybe we should give it a home. Perhaps later we can go and look for it and if it's in the police kennels maybe they'll let us have it if no one claims it."

"I reckon it was a stray, I said. No collar, scruffy, a bit mucky as if it had been sleeping rough."

"That's my dog," Luckry chirped. "It's my friend. Big Gran said."

I couldn't help a sigh. "I keep telling you, Big Gran is dead."

Luckry turned her big brown eyes onto me in a pitying way. "Big Gran talks to me a lot. She told me to go back to the well and that you'd come for me and to keep as dry as I could, which I couldn't really."

"Luckry," I asked. "Why did you really go back to the well?"

"Because Big Gran told me to, I just said."

"Yes, but what had you to do?"

"I threw in the wrong coin. It was a big wish, a very big one, so Big Gran said I had to throw in a big coin. I thought she meant her big coin but she meant a £2 piece. She said you'd be angry when you found I'd put in the wrong coin and so would Mum and Dad so when everything started shaking and I couldn't do my pumps, I climbed out of the classroom window as everyone else was in the hall and I did what Big Gran told me – I went back to get it."

She explained about meeting the shopper who'd asked her if she was OK. "I looked down the top of the well and I thought I could see it but I couldn't get the top off. Big Gran told me to go to the far side and there was an old grate thing and I tugged at it and the doggie tugged at the padlock as well and the padlock broke and the grate thing came up. I could see the stream and Big Gran said to try to crawl along it and I did but it was very cold. Suddenly, the stream went down a hill and I slipped and fell and banged my mouth."

We turned off London road onto the road which would eventually get us to the Traveller site.

"The water sort of pushed me – I think it was the water but it might have been Big Gran."

"What, in that pipe?" I asked incredulously. "Big Gran was a round fat woman ..."

"Oy," Mum snapped. "We'll have a bit of respect if you don't mind."

"Sorry, I just meant that she couldn't have got into a pipe even if she'd been alive."

"Big Gran's like a sort of angel," Luckry explained. "You can't see her at all, you just know she's there and you can hear her talking to you. She told me to pick up her coin and I put it in my pocket. I wanted to take some of the other coins as well but Big Gran said I couldn't as they were other peoples' wishes but it was all right to take my wish back but not to touch theirs."

"Quite right," Mum said. "It'd be very wrong to steal someone's things. I found Big Gran's coin in your soggy socks of all places, as well as some more money and £15 in notes.

"There were no pockets in my PE shorts," she explained.

We turned off the road and into the lane which led directly to the site. There were still people standing at the entrance and I could see TV cameras and people I thought must be Press.

"What did you want the £15 for?" I asked.

"To buy you a present to make you happier," said Luckry. We pulled up outside our trailer. I felt like the day had just collapsed because it was the proof that I had been the cause of the whole mess.

Thirty Eight

I can't say I've ever been really depressed before. I've had times when I've been very unhappy, like when I got the burns at Marshall Meadows, or when they teased and – well, bullied me – at school. There were times I just didn't want to face having to go to school, when I cried about it but Mum made me go, times when she went to school, and spoke to teachers about what the other kids were doing to me. They were horrible times but this felt much worse because my baby sister, who I love to bits, felt she had to spend money to me to keep in with me – to 'make me happier', as she put it.

I sat in the far corner of the trailer on one of the fold down seat beds as visitor after visitor from the site came round to say how great it was that we were all OK and hadn't I done well. They brought me little gifts – and plenty for Luckry of course – and pressed them on me, like chocolate bars and bags of sweets and Uncle Arthur gave me his old flower knife and said that now I had proved myself a man I should learn to use a knife correctly and make things with it like our people used to do in the past and still do sometimes, because it's a good way of earning a bit of money in a crisis.

Another time I'd have thought the knife was a terrific thing but the way I was feeling then it was anything but. What I really wanted to do was to go off on my own and try to sort myself out, or maybe go and see Nat and spend some time with her because Nat would know the right things to say to cheer me up, though she'd probably give me a slap, too.

I think Mum saw I was down in the dumps because when the visitors cleared a bit she came and sat next to me and put her arm round me. "You know, son," she said. "After what you've gone through you've had a big shock to the system and all the stress and all the worry and fears can bubble up and make you feel rotten despite all the good things you've done."

I couldn't speak, I just nodded. "Listen, son," she said. "Why not go for a little walk round?"

I shook my head. "There's all Press outside the site and people gawping. You know what the Press is like with Travellers, I just don't want to have to go past them and have them snapping cameras and phones at me and shouting and wanting me to talk and following me and trying to rile me so that I say or do the wrong thing and then they print something or show it on telly so everyone can say, 'Typical Traveller – no such thing as a good one.'"

Mum nodded. "I understand, well, why not go and sit on the grass? Find some of the others and go for a chat."

I knew where she meant. About half the site is bounded by Marshall Meadows – there's grass there, but that's not what she meant, of course. The rest of the site has those high bankings round so that people in houses don't have to look at the dirty decadent Diddies. If you cross the site diagonally from our trailer, you get to a banking which blocks the view from some bungalows on the edge of a social housing estate and if you go up the banking and down the far side, you're on a different road altogether and the grass there – my Dad cuts it – is nice and clean.

"You could call for Sammy Green," Mum suggested.

Sammy's another Romany boy on the site, one who doesn't go to school and he and I get on and Luckry sometimes plays with his kid sisters.

It was something to do, something to take my mind off things because I couldn't speak to Mum about how guilty I felt. "Yeah," I said. I picked my way past visitors' knees and precariously balanced cups of tea – mengri we call it – and out of the trailer. I crossed diagonally to No. 8. Actually, we don't have numbers on the trailer plots officially, but Dad gave them all numbers to make it easier when he was writing down who'd paid rent and what not when he collected the money for the council.

No one was in at No. 8 – their work van wasn't parked there and I guessed the whole family must have gone out in it somewhere. *Just my luck,* I thought. *What now?*

Thirty Nine

Dejectedly, I went between two trailer caravans and up the banking, dropping down on the far side so that I overlooked the bungalows. I sat with my legs downhill. Mum didn't like us going there as sometimes the people in the houses'd come out and shout insults at us and tell us to get back down our holes, only they used four letter words as well. I've heard lots of bad language, don't get me wrong, but Mum says it isn't proper and no one'd better use it anywhere near her. If Dad forgets himself sometimes because something's gone wrong, Mum really gives it to him.

I was doing no harm sitting on the banking. Sometimes, one or two of the lads from the site will shout back if they're insulted and their language would make a bull blush, but all I wanted to do was sit quietly and try to get my mind back in order. I pulled a few blades of grass unthinkingly, and wondered how I could ever make things right with Luckry for having been so horrible and causing it all.

Something prodded me in the ribs.

"Oh no, not you." The scruffy dog had nosed me and was now dancing about and sneezing in its excitement as if it had found a long lost friend. I patted it and rubbed its ears and it seemed to like that. I wished I'd had a biscuit or something to give it.

"What's to do then dog, eh?" I asked it. It sneezed again and pushed into me with its nose.

Something slumped down against my other side. I turned to find Luckry.

"Hello," she said. "Hello big brother."

Through my sadness I couldn't help a little smile.

"Hello, little sister," I rejoined.

She pulled a sweet out of a big bag and thrust it into my mouth. "I love you," she said.

I couldn't stop the tears. They rushed up like a fountain, bubbled like the water in the well, shook me like the quake. They flowed down my face and dripped to my chin. The dog on one side of me tried to lick my face, but I stopped it, whilst Luckry on the other threw her little arms round me and hugged me as best she could.

"It's all right, big brother," she said. "Big Gran says you're a hero."

"But I'm not," I protested through my tears. "I caused it – I was horrible to you and then you felt you had to put yourself in danger, all because of me and the wish and then go back for the wrong coin."

Luckry whispered, "But really it was all my fault."

I must have looked confused because I felt it. Of course it wasn't. "What? Your fault? But how?"

Her swollen lips quavered. "It was the pumps. The wish!"

"Yeah!" I agreed. "I know you made a wish but I don't get you because it was my fault actually, you wouldn't even have had to go through it all if I'd done the right thing and gone into school with you and sorted your PE pumps out."

"It was cos I wished. I didn't want to do PE, so I wished … I wished …"

Her voice wavered on the brink of tears.

"I wished for something to happen so I didn't have to do PE and the pumps! And it did!"

The tears came. Now it was my turn to snuggle Luckry to me, whilst the dog had changed sides and gone to her licky aid as well.

"Oh no!" I said. "All cos I was grumpy about the pumps! So now you think you caused the earthquake to dodge PE! Course you didn't!"

"You know my wishes? At the Magic Well? Well, I made two."

"Two? You only threw one coin, Big Gran's."

"No, I threw another coin as well, it was a £2 one. The second one came true, too," she said. "Know what it was?"

"No – ouch!" I banged a sore bit on my hand on the banking.

"For you to be nice to me about the pumps. And you were, Blotch. You were really smashing. You did much more than the pumps! Mum says you saved my life!"

"Cos you're my kid sister, that's my job!" I said simply.

"Yeah!" she agreed. And she chuckled.

"And I found your silver horse hair slide – that lady shopper had it!" She almost cheered. "It's back in the trailer," I said.

I felt much happier suddenly.

Forty

We walked back over the green barrier and across the site hand in hand, a loving brother and sister, the latter with the scruffy dog seemingly fastened to her leg, and stopped in the middle of the site because something was happening. Men were piling wood and putting a stockpile nearby and I guessed why.

Years ago, when Romany people were travelling about, they lived with a fire wherever they stopped. It was used for cooking and socialising and it'd be lit first thing in a morning and kept lit all day and into the night because, when we lived in tents, the fire would be at the mouth of the tent to provide some warmth and tired people could come home to a quick meal. You're fairly limited what you can cook on a fire when you have to carry all your cooking utensils on a donkey or your own back.

Even though we're on a site, the yag is still important but we tend to only have one on special occasions like the night before a funeral or wedding or to celebrate a birth or a christening or a special event.

Granny Raini was sitting in her trailer with her massive black pot on the ground in front of her and she was busy peeling and chopping up lots of vegetable. Other people were spreading bits of old matting and boxes and garden chairs in a big circle round the future fire. Uncle Arthur hammered a kekkavi saster into the ground so the hook of the kettle iron was over the fire to hang a kettle off it. Someone else put up a three-legged tripod (we call it a chitty) to hold a pot. It was all very new to Luckry but not to me.

One of the ladies set up trestle tables with white cloths on and before long a range of puddings began to appear on it, carefully protected by food covers or upturned dishes. Piles of Crown Derby dishes went alongside.

"Is it for me?" Luckry asked.

"In a way," I said. "But really it's for everyone. You were in danger and I was in danger but we're both OK and safe, so we have a Romani party for a special occasion because everyone is glad it's turned out OK."

Dusk came at last and with it, the lighting of the fire. I wanted to do it, but Uncle Arthur insisted.

"You been in enough danger for a lifetime," he asserted, as if I was going to find striking a match risky.

Once the blaze was going, Gran Raini's big old pot was hung on the tripod and a blackened kettle on the kettle saster. People began to assemble round the fire, sitting on the old boxes, on oil drums or even the occasional old chair – Karen, who hadn't yet left in her caravan, was given an old home-made wicker chair just right for a respected visitor. Luckry sat on a rug between Mum and

Dad with me next to Dad and the mutt dog nuzzled in behind Luckry.

There was a lot of laughter, a lot of jokes and some hand warming at the fire that wasn't strictly necessary, though I did it, too, as it seemed to be the right thing. Someone had brought some brandy and someone whisky – they each said they'd got 'an awful thirst' and the bottles got passed round the men without any glasses but polystyrene cups. I was offered it but didn't, though I saw Sammy Green take a big swig of the brandy then his face changed and he started a huge coughing fit, *Serves you right*, I thought.

Mum fetched an iron frying pan and put a huge steak in it. "That for me?" Dad asked, but she didn't reply. It took a long time for the stew to be declared ready and by the time it was, the steak was also done. Some of the ladies began spooning out the stew from the big pot and bowls were passed round together with a big hunk of bread each. Dad took an exceptionally large hunk of bread, eyeing the steak. As Mum used a slice to get the steak out, he held out a hunk of bread split down the middle for her to slip the steak in.

"Not for you," she said. I wondered if I'd be the lucky one – we don't have it often. "Pass me a knife." I'd got the flower knife Uncle Arthur gave me safe in my belt in a sheath so I passed it. Carefully, she chopped the steak up into little bits, blowing on them almost hard enough to blow them off the frying pan slice.

"What you doing?" Dad asked.

"Not for you," Mum said. "For the fourth hero. Here, Luckry, give these cooler bits to the dog."

The dog dropped what it had been carrying since we left the well yesterday – Nat's scarf, very soggy looking.

"Hey!" Dad protested but I knew it was for effect and everyone round the fire was laughing at the notion that Dad had just been done out of his steak. Other dogs on the site crept forward at the smell but they didn't get a look in.

Forty One

As I say, it's not often we have a bari yag like this. The last one I remember was for Big Gran the night before her funeral, so that was sort of much more sombre. There was still a lot of laughter then because Romany people have to keep laughing or they'd cry, Mum says, and there's always music. Someone had an old fiddle, someone a squeezebox and a couple of people had guitars and after a bit of a hoo-ha about whose instrument was correctly tuned and whose wasn't, the music got going. Uncle Harry Finney played the spoons. Granny Raini gave a super display of step dancing, which is as lot more difficult than it looks. We sang lovely old Gypsy songs, some sad, some happy and some, sort of, saying how clever we are to survive in a world which doesn't want us. Some of our songs are very old about transportation, slavery and hangings of innocent people for being Romani.

There's lots of stories, too – old folk tales, hundreds of them that have been told round the fire for centuries, including several you house people think are your stories but which you actually got from us – yes, that's true. Granny Raini is a great story teller and she has a ruby red velvet purse with brass clasps on the top and claims that she keeps all her old stories in there, so if you ask her for one she opens it and reckons to search inside for a suitable one. She told several crackers. As the evening got later, I saw that Luckry was fast asleep, full to the brim with stew and stories, and Mum had wrapped her up in the blanket and was holding her to herself whilst the dog sat close by on guard.

The music changed to hymns because several of the people on the site have found God and got converted and some of those hymns are even about Travellers so they're especially popular with us all.

My own eyes were starting to droop and several of the other youngsters were already zonked like Luckry when I felt a hand on my shoulder. It was Granny Raini, beckoning me to follow.

She led me over to the far side of the site, if you imagine it's like the most North Westerly corner and pointed over the fence into Marshall Meadows.

"Big Gran wants to talk to you," she said. "She can't get you to here when you're in all that noise by the fire. E's 'ere now," she said, talking into the dark.

I couldn't see Big Gran at all, no semi ghostly shape or anything, but I sensed her there and I could hear her voice – weird, I know – not like before when I only thought she had given me an idea to go and find Luckry at the school. This time it was an actual voice.

"I cun see 'im, I cun see 'im," came the irritated voice of Big Gran from nowhere. I peered but there was no figure, no ghost, no one in the moonlight, just a voice without a body. "Now listen you 'ere, young Blotch Morrison, dere's two things you got to do."

I was astonished when I heard what the two things were. "But I haven't got any money," I protested.

"No, not yet, but you will have," she said. "I knows about dese things. You listen to your ole Big Gran."

"So do I sell the gold coins you left us to get the money?"

"O'course not, fool," her voice sounding scornful. "You'll not need to. De money's a-comin' to you in only a few days. Mark my words. I tole you about the big needles and the earth not a-liking it, and was I right? Course I was right. Now you got to *do* the right thing for de kiddies on this site an' for your Natalie girl an' you go tell everyone round dat fire what you got to do so they all helps you."

"I'll try," I said.

"You're a good chavi, young Blotch," she said.

"How do you do that? How do you make your voice come like that even though you're dead and buried and you haven't got a voice any more?" I asked. There was no answer, so I asked again.

"Fool," said Granny Raini. "She's not 'ere now. She's gone, so just do as she told you, that's all."

The air felt cold and a shiver ran down my back, my hands were shaking too. I stumbled back to the fire, longing for some warmth, Granny Raini following some distance behind and I slumped down beside Dad. Then I cleared my throat and said I had an announcement from Big Gran and told the people what she had told me she wanted me to do.

Forty Two

It was ten minutes before 11 p.m. when I began to tell them what Big Gran's plan was and as I finished, I heard a distant church clock strike the hour. In actual fact, it was nothing to do with them what big Gran wanted doing, well, not really, but she'd wanted me to talk to everyone about it. I felt proud that she'd trusted me so much – in fact, proud, too, when I thought about it that she'd also trusted me earlier to save Luckry and to speak on her behalf to everyone round the fire.

At first, there was absolute silence, and for a moment I thought they were going to be against and that I'd made a fool of myself. Then murmurs of support began and the few older kids still awake thought it was a brilliant plan.

By ten past everyone was in agreement, though I was still worried about where the money was going to come from. At that point, Karen said she thought we'd better not play any more music for fear of disturbing the people on the social housing estate. Someone called for a last go at the religious song, As I was a-walking one morning in Spring, I met with some Travellers in an old country lane

... It's a lovely one and I admit we were singing it louder than perhaps we should, or maybe it was the whisky and the brandy that the men had had which made it rowdier. Uncle Charlie Gaskin had just played the last chord when there was a bang like a gun going off. Everyone went absolutely quiet, then we could hear Charlie's mum, Lizzie, sort of moaning and going, "Ooo, ooo," then, "Help, help," very weakly.

Uncle Charlie ran from the fire and across the site to his mum's trailer and several more men, including Dad, as well as Karen ran, too, so I followed. Aunt Lizzie stood in the doorway, holding onto the doorframe like grim death. Uncle Charlie was trying to help her out of the trailer but she seemed to be so frightened she just clung to the door frame and wouldn't let go. A cool breeze had come up by then and she was only in a long flannel nightie and slippers and shaking. I'd like to say like a leaf but this was a shudder-shake and it was so bad you could hear her teeth clacking together.

Everyone was asking her what had happened but she simply couldn't speak. Uncle Charlie lifted her from the trailer and carried her away in his arms to his own trailer to give her a warm drink and find what the problem was. Old ladies – and she didn't know her age any more than we did but we reckoned 70s-80s – don't fare well when attacked.

Actually, you could get a good idea what had gone off – lying on the floor, right next to her bed, was a large stone with a piece of paper wrapped round it. Yes, the sort of thing you only hear about in books but it's something we Travellers experience from time to time. Dad went into the trailer and picked it up. It was a large stone which had knocked out an entire trailer window and its inner frame and cracked and frosted the glass but without actually breaking it because most of the glass in trailers these days is safety glass. Good thing too.

Karen shouted, "Finger prints!" but Dad was already holding the rock and pulling the paper, which was held on with an elastic band. He realised and sheepishly and gingerly handed it over to Karen, who had put on forensic gloves and who waggled the note into an evidence bag.

"Doubt if we'll get anything from the stone, she said, And probably not the paper either. I expect they knew to be careful."

"Sorry," said Dad. "I never thought. It must have been thrown from the road. Someone from the social housing I expect."

"Did you read it?" I asked. Dad's one of the very few older people on the site who can actually read. Most people have to get a child to read something for them.

"Not exactly, but it was something about shut the eff up, effing Pikeys and get back down the rat-holes where you belong."

"We'll obviously try to find who was responsible," said Karen as we walked back to the fire. "But ..."

"But you won't succeed," I finished for her.

"I was going to say it wouldn't be easy," she said, giving me a look.

Nobody wanted to sit by the fire any more. Mum had carried Luckry back to our home for safety and had tucked her into bed, though whether anywhere was safe with people chucking stones into homes I wasn't at all sure.

A couple of men came back who'd been searching down the road but they found no one.

"There's no CCTV either," said Dad. "So no chance for you police. They must have lobbed the stone from the top of the banking at the first caravan they saw and it was just bad luck it was Aunt Lizzie's. We should have packed in the music earlier."

"It may have been more to do with jealousy at the attention you've all been getting." Karen peeled off the forensic gloves and scrunched them into a ball to throw in the bin. The music wasn't that loud.

Forty Three

On the Saturday, the day after the fire and the stone, I went to Nat's house (uninvited). You'll probably ask why I didn't phone first but I don't have a mobile phone – I know I must be the only person in the world who hasn't – but I haven't because Mum and Dad say they can't afford it and it'd only get nicked at school. If you're a Traveller, you're fair game. I've lost loads of football shorts and boots as they think it's funny to take them from my bag and chuck them in the school bins or up into telephone wires. So Mum and Dad are probably right. Why don't I what? Well, I'm tempted to give them a good smack but I know that if I did it'd be me got suspended because it's very strict at my school about not using violence for any reason whatsoever, but not so strict about losing people's things for them. I've got my own way of dealing with things – for instance, I put a Gypsy curse on Jack Wignall. Of course, it wasn't real but it was about spiders so every time he saw one for weeks, he thought it was the curse. That made a few people think and quietened things down for a while. I don't know how Luckry will cope when she gets there – mind, she does have Big Gran.

Anyway, it was because of what Big Gran said that I needed to see Nat urgently and it wouldn't wait until Monday. I took her sister's soggy college scarf with me (though later Mum said she'd have washed it if I'd reminded her). I could have used the site's council phone from the tiny office next to our trailers to ring first but it's only for official site use and I wasn't sure I should for this. I thought maybe 9 a.m. was a bit early for Nat but when I got to Willow Rise I saw that the curtains were open so I risked her wrath. Nat herself opened the door to me.

"Nat," I asked cautiously. "Could we have a private chat?"

"What?" she asked.

"I wondered if I could have a word, like very privately, where" (and I mouthed 'your parents') "can't hear?"

"Ooo," came her dad's voice from the living room, "we can't hear from here."

Nat went beetroot. "Wait there," she said, and fetched her coat. "I'm going for a walk, WITH TOM!" she almost shouted and slammed the front door. "Where we going?" she asked, zipping up her hoody.

"Could we go to the site?"

"The site? Private? People are in and out the whole time there."

"I wondered about us going and sitting on the banking, you know, where the social housing is."

She gave me a funny look. "I don't know what this is about, Thomas Morrison, but it'd better be a good reason.

My parents'll tease me to death when I get back home as it is so if it's not a good reason, you know what to expect."

I did.

We walked mainly in agonised silence except I noticed she no longer had the bandage on and that only one of her plaits was fastened to the side of her French-plait style, but the other wasn't a plait, just hanging loose hair. She saw me looking at it. The bandage was a nuisance, she explained curtly.

When we reached the green banking, we flopped down side by side. I wasn't sure how to raise it. I began by telling her about the big fire we had and about the stone incident and we looked from the top of the banking at Aunt Lizzie's caravan where the knocked-out window had been temporarily replaced with a board. I gave her a carrier bag with the soggy scarf and she chuckled.

Then I told her about Big Gran talking to me. I thought Nat would figure I was crazy or just a stupidly superstitious Gyppo. I so wanted to hold her hand but I daren't. I wasn't worried if she hit me, but I was worried she might never want to be my friend again.

"Big Gran wanted me to do something, well two things actually but only one is to do with you."

"Oh?"

I put my hand on the grass and edged it towards hers, millimetres at a time. "You know she left twelve Victorian £5 pieces for her great grandchildren? Of course, Luckry still has hers despite using it for the big wish and mine is safe, too, but one coin never went to anyone. It should have gone to our Ruby, but she died the day she was born.

Mum and Dad kept it in case they ever have another child, a brother or a sister to me and Luckry, but Mum says that can't happen now. Well, Big Gran said – and I asked everyone round the fire and they all agreed – she said, she wanted you to have the twelfth coin."

"Me? Oh no, I couldn't."

"Oh but you see we all want you to. Romany kids don't get many friends from you house dwellers, you gorjers, we call you. Everyone wants you to have it" – my fingers touched her hand – "You see, you're not just a friend, you feel like my sister – I mean as well as Luckry." I got hold of two of her fingers. "Please Nat, we want you to have it."

"But I'm friends with you because of who you are, not because of any old coin."

"Yes, I know that – you didn't even know about the coin until Luckry and the well. But we put a big store by people who feel more like brothers and sisters who aren't. Well, you know that's true – all people older than we are we call Aunt or Uncle and Romanies we're not related to, except very distantly, we usually call Cous. Will you accept it? You're my best friend in all the world and no one else would have stood by me like you did – you're a true sister to me and to Luckry."

She was silent for a moment.

"Please, we all want it."

I expected her to say something about not listening to imaginary dead Grandmas but she didn't. "I'll have to ask my parents."

"Yes of course."

She took my entire hand in hers and squeezed it twice.

"If they agree – I think they will when I explain – it'd be an honour and I promise you that I'll keep it for ever. A token of trust between people of two ethnic groups."

She leaned over towards me and kissed me on the cheek. I pulled my hand away and started to put it round her waist because I wanted to kiss her properly.

"Don't be silly, she said. Brothers and sisters don't snog," and kissed me again on the cheek.

Afterword

Karen had decided to stay a couple days more because of the stone throwing and she told me then that it was her who recommended to the Chief Constable that Nat and I be put forward for an award for saving the dinner lady and, of course, saving Luckry. I know it was me went down the actual pipe but I couldn't have done any of it without Nat. I wish she knew how much I care about her and that I know that the slaps she gives are her way of showing affection. DON'T PRINT THAT!

Aunt Lizzie had a massive bruise on her leg where the stone had hit her but worse, it was a long time before she dared stay in that trailer at night, though she's OK now. Someone's lent her a big klaxon horn with a squeezy rubber on the end and when you squeeze it, it sounds like a ship hooting. She hasn't needed to use it yet and the window's fixed. By the way, the police never found the stone thrower – I knew they wouldn't.

They've put a new manhole cover over the pipe now and it's got the biggest padlock you've ever seen. There's a new mesh grill over the top, too, and that's also got a huge new padlock. Tell you what, they'd need something stronger than fire service bolt cutters to get through it another time, but it's still a wishing well. There's also still a big patch of nettles though – I reckon they've left them to deter people from having a go.

You'll know about the money, of course. Your £10,000 for this series of magazine articles, well it came to me, or rather, Mum and Dad for me. But I said I wanted to do with it what Big Gran had told me. So now, look, over there, in the corner of the site where Big Gran spoke to me, they're just beginning building a little kiddies' play area. The people who own Marshall Meadows gave a piece to the council to be part of the site. It was a bit where there'd never been any chemicals, only green grass and they moved their fence back and built it massively higher (to stop balls) so we've got like a wedge of land added to the site with a grassy play area, two swings, a slide, a play caravan and one of those parallel bar things for hanging off with safe play surfaces underneath them all – or rather, we will have when it's finished. The money's paying for the play equipment and its erection.

I'll tell you one thing, though. I know you'll think it's weird about Big Gran talking to Luckry and me and even Granny Raini, but I've wondered and worried a bit about one thing. Luckry wanted to miss out on PE and she wished for something to happen that would get her out of it – a big wish. Well, you can't have a much bigger answer to a wish than an earthquake. So I've been worrying that Big Gran might even have caused that earthquake. Mum says I'm being ridiculous.

Oh look, here's the mutt now. Of course we adopted him, well, it was the least we could do, especially after he'd wolfed down Dad's steak. Not really – for what he did for Luckry, of course. Take his picture, too. Meet Quake ... Winner of the Morrisons' Meat Medal.

Talking of names, Dad also wanted to change my sis Luckry's name to Lickry and call her that, but Mum gave him a severe warning. So she's still Luckry – Lucretia. And I love my little sis to bits.

Ends